8.20 - 9:30 วัน 9. June

Finley's Christmas Secret

EMMA HARDWICK

Drina
ROMANCE
PUBLISHING

COPYRIGHT

Title: Finley's Christmas Secret

First published in 2021

The author and the publisher specifically disclaim any liability, loss or risk which is incurred as a consequence, directly or indirectly, of the use and application of any contents of this work.

CONTENTS

1

FINLEY

Close to the fall of darkness, eight-year-old Finley Harrington struggled against the howling wind. Her hands and face were dirty, and she looked dog-tired as she staggered along, dragging her dress in the mud. The first drops of heavy rain fell, stinging her face and mixing with her tears. Although she didn't have far to go, she would be drenched when she got home. In the biting cold, her fingers had ached around the joints before they went pale and numb. A hard day's labour in the fields had exhausted the poor girl, so much so she could barely stand. She did her best to look like she was helping but really was marking time until the terrible toil could end. Her brothers were still busy, heads down grafting away, but Lester, the eldest who always kept an eye out for her, felt sorry for his little sister.

"Why not go into the farmhouse and warm up in front of the fire? You've done enough for today, Fin."

The summer had been hard that year, and her army colonel father was counting on her and her brothers to take care of the family farmstead while he was away on campaign. Ernest had insisted that they leave the crop as long as they could in the hope that something could be harvested. His plan failed. The family had waited far too long, and the crop lay dead and wizened. The soil was water-logged, and soon the ground would be frozen.

Although Finley was only eight, she knew what a blow this would be for the family and that her father was in some far-off country, unable to provide for them. Finley lived in constant terror that her father wouldn't return. What if this dreadful war stole her beloved pa from her?

It had not always been like this. There was a time when life was better.

*

Captain Ernest Harrington met his wife Emma at an officer's ball in London. She was a shy young lady, soft and lovely. Emma was the antithesis of war. She was beautiful, tender, soothing. She brought about a sense of peace and comfort for his tortured soul. Her family accepted him because he was a young captain with a good future. In return, Ernest's family welcomed Emma, so beautiful, socially acceptable, and rich. The news of the engagement brought relief to his beleaguered father, terrified that his son would settle with a lowly woman on some exotic far-flung shore.

Just like little Finley, Emma suffered the endless fear that her husband would die. Captain Harrington moved from campaign to campaign. His commanders always persuaded him to do one last battle, as he was a competent leader and a respected officer. It didn't cross their minds that Ernest was as vulnerable as everybody else. As a man, he had tremendous empathy for the young cavalry officers under his command. He would return to the firing line, having convinced himself that he could save their lives with his experience. He would convince Emma of the same and promise her that this was the last time he would leave her.

Ernest and Emma started a family. After giving her husband four robust sons, she gave birth to a daughter. Ernest's family was his delight. All of his brood gave him a sense of true fulfilment.

"We can't call her Finley," Emma chided her husband." It is an absurd name for a girl."

"Of course we can! She is going to be a warrior! Look at those little fists," he laughed in protest.

"Then, Finley she shall be. If it pleases you."

She smiled at him lovingly.

"I can't wait to put her on a horse," said Ernest.

"You will do no such thing!" Emma Harrington warned with a grin. "I have waited many years to have a daughter. You have four sons to keep yourself busy with. This baby is mine."

From that moment forward, mother and daughter were inseparable.

*

For the umpteenth Christmas in their marriage, Emma would be alone in the church with her children. The lone parent put on a brave face, but inside she was gloomy. Looking at her cherished little ones, all she wished for was that their father be home to share the joy of the day with them. Still an infant, Finley had rarely seen her father. With a deep breath and a bright smile, Emma entered the church for the Christmas morning service. No one knew that dark thoughts dwelled within her.

The day was one of the coldest Emma had ever experienced. Ice hung from every rail, gutter, and gable. The yuletide service ended with a rapturous rendition of 'O Holy Night'. Bursting into song with the congregation filled her with some of the joy that she lacked. After ensuring the children were well covered, she jostled them toward the coach.

"Come on, now. Keep together."

"Yes, ma!" they chorused.

Two streets away, Bill Benson climbed off his cart. It had been a long shift for the weary man. The recent cold snap had brought a huge demand for coal, and he had made deliveries throughout the night. Finally, he reached the huge gates where he stabled his horse. It wouldn't be long now until he could go home to his wife and two children. All he wanted to do was sit down and have a cup of hot tea to thaw him.

"You've done well today, Stanley Benson. Very well indeed," said Bill, patting the Clydesdale's muscular neck.

As he walked off to swing the doors open, the horse waited patiently for its master, knowing he was at his stable. Soon, he, too, would be warm and fed.

The sun had risen, and the meagre light lifted the temperature by a few degrees. High above, a large glistening stalactite slowly began to drip. Soon, the weakest point couldn't support the frozen weight below. The rod of ice snapped with the crack of a branch and plummeted towards the cart. It landed like an exploding bomb, terrifying the huge creature.

The horse reared in fear and bolted, dragging the heavy cart behind it. The cart's brakes were on, and the wrenching squeal of steel-on-steel tormented the stallion even more. Traumatised, the animal turned into the same street as the church, out of control, thundering down the icy lane. Far behind, dashed a helpless Bill Benson, yelling out for the horse to stop, but to no avail.

At the same moment, Emma reached the coach with her children. Out of the corner of her eye, she saw a little boy blindly run into the street. In the distance, she heard the clatter of horseshoes on cobbles, high pitched screeching brakes and iron wheels. The racket scared Finley. She looked up to Lester for reassurance, who took her hand and squeezed it until her knuckles almost cracked. With his other arm, he ushered his siblings out of the way until they had their backs up against the coach and feet on tiptoes.

"Come here, lad. Quickly now," said Emma outstretching her arm as her gaze flitted between the boy and the cart.

Fear rooted the youngster to the spot.

"Slow down, Sir!" shrieked the young mother. "Stop!"

It was then she realised there was no driver. The colossal beast charged down the middle of the street. Instinct propelled Emma forward. She ran to the boy. As she reached him, the horse was almost on top of them. Emma dived forward and pushed the child so hard that he went sprawling onto the opposite pavement. The bystanders gasped. Emma tried to stand up, but the smooth soles of her leather boots slipped on the icy cobbles. She lay sprawled on the street as the ground trembled like an earthquake. It was too late. She knew she was going to die. Lifting her head, she saw her five children standing watching, paralysed and helpless.

The horse hit her slight frame. Its great hooves crushed her skull. The cart followed and broke the bones in her body. The four little boys didn't move. They just stared at their mother, too shocked to speak.

Finley began to scream and ran towards Emma. The coachman tried to stop her, but she wriggled away from him.

"Oh, Mama! Wake up, Mama!" she cried, then begged, "Please!"

Emma Harrington would never wake up again.

Poor Finley was just four years old.

2

FROM CAPTAIN TO COLONEL

Lester Harrington watched his sister charging down the old farmhouse stairs, shaking his head and smiling to himself. At twenty-one years old, she was beautiful, wild, and most definitely independent. Finley was wearing a simple dress with no bustles underneath the skirt. She hated the ridiculous whale-bone hoops around her body.

> "It makes me feel as if I am trapped in a birdcage," she would remonstrate when challenged about it.

As much as her brothers were protective of her, their Ernest had raised them to appreciate that what was good for the geese was good for the gander. The sight of many brave women coping with the horrors of war had taught the down-to-earth colonel just how resourceful they could be.

Finley's long hair was loose and hung down her back like a shimmering waterfall. Her eyes flashed with determination, and her broad smile belied her steely will. Despite the tough start, she had a contagious joy that followed her wherever she went. She saw the humour in everything.

The Harringtons were a lovely bunch, but more so, Finley. The upper-class young ladies in the area stuck their noses up at her, but try as they might, they couldn't deny Finley's natural grace, akin to that of a ballet dancer.

Lester couldn't believe that this was once the little girl who would do back-breaking work with her brothers. Some people had suggested that Finley go to a convent after Emma died, but Ernest and his sons wouldn't hear of it, so decided to employ a governess for Finley. With the help of the small band of household staff, the girl was well-cared for.

*

It was Miss Reeves, Finley's governess, who had the determination to grow her confidence. The girl's tutor relished the opportunity to develop an over-privileged young woman into a caring, empathetic soul who could respect her position and use it for good. So, between her father's leadership and Rebecca Reeves's wisdom, Finley was taught to think critically, not a skill akin to most privileged Victorian women.

"Finley, one day, you will need the strong character that people criticise you for. Don't listen to a word of gossip. Participate in these events as a distant observer, and never compare yourself to anybody else," Miss Reeves advised.

Ernest had spotted that Rebecca had a good sense of humour, a craving for adventure and the energy to match Finley. He knew they were the perfect partnership.

As a military father away on tours of duty, Ernest didn't interfere very much with his daughter's education. He allowed Miss Reeves to do exactly as she pleased, extremely glad that there was someone to educate Finley in 'feminine matters'. The idea of his daughter's transition to womanhood filled him with trepidation, and he found it reprehensible that he should play any part in explaining her physical transformation.

"It is out of the question," he told Rebecca.

Finley was devastated when she had her first menses at thirteen. She felt as if her carefree life had reached an end and resented her body for humiliating her. Clenching her fists in a temper, she thumped them against her belly.

"I won't be able to do anything," she cried in frustration. "I'll be forced to sit about while the boys have fun. I won't be able to ride or take part in any outdoor activities."

"Shush now. Stop lamenting about your condition," ordered Miss Reeves. "You are not the only woman in the world who suffers this every month. It may be seen as a natural disaster for some people, but you will not allow it to rule your life. I won't tolerate you moping about. We'll make the best of this inconvenient situation, and you will do everything that you love."

Miss Reeves was as good as her word. Finley listened to the woman's stern advice and refused to have the dreaded curse determine her lifestyle. In turn, Miss Reeves assisted her in managing her hygiene in a manner that allowed her to continue riding, fencing, and hunting.

Her brothers often brought their friends home. At first, these young chaps were intrigued by such a beautiful girl, but when she began beating them at chess, croquet or showed them up for their poor horsemanship, they would sulk and never return. Finley didn't understand why boys found it offensive to compete with girls. She was in a home, far away in the rolling countryside, where no restrictions were placed upon her. She had no idea of a woman's place in a man's world. She wasn't educated to know the difference.

*

Colonel Harrington remarried around the time of Finley's fifteenth birthday. As a rule, he only noted campaign dates in his calendar, not birthdays. When he arrived home with his new bride, Finley cut the delicious cake that the cook had made her.

"It is untoward for young ladies to slice cake. You should have a servant doing it," were Eleanor's first words to her stepdaughter.

Finley gave Eleanor a cool stare. The new woman in the Harrington household didn't realise that she had made an enemy for life. Before excusing themselves, Cook and Miss Reeves made themselves busy, pretending to tidy up the spotless kitchen.

Later, Finley complained to her father.

"She is horrid, unkind, and you will be sorry that you ever married her! You mark my words."

"You just got off to a bad start. Eleanor has tremendous social skills, Finley. You need a woman to steer through all this society nonsense coming up in a few years. You might have grown up in a bubble living here, but at some point, you will need to leave the nest and learn the ways of the wider world."

*

After Colonel Harrington's promotion, the family was forced to become more socially correct. Much against her will, Finley was presented at court.

"For once, you will have to do something that you don't like, my girl!"

"I am not a horse, father. I don't wish to be paraded so that the best bull can decide they want to breed with me," she protested.

"Now, you listen up. I will not tolerate your insolence, and I find your observation crass. Find a pretty dress and put a feather in your hair. Then get on with the show."

Colonel Harrington agreed with his daughter's complaint. The ridiculous process was absurd—but he couldn't tell her so in case Eleanor was listening.

*

Finley was a disastrous debutante. Although the most beautiful young woman of the season, the soft young men who tried to court her were always disappointed. No man could hold her interest for long. Her suitors ranged from overconfident university students to young industrial men desperate to copulate as soon as they could find a willing victim.

Never cruel, she preferred to be elusive. Her health always seemed to fail during the season as she succumbed to a few critical but fleeting illnesses. One example was the excruciating, unrelenting migraines, which kept her in bed for days. These sporadic episodes usually coincided with one other social ceremony or another.

Her father didn't care what she did, but her stepmother was outraged. She longed to march Finley all over London and force her to suffer polite weekends at the homes of the well-to-do. Eleanor would grab the girl by the elbow and deliver whispered reprimands.

"You are the only woman I know who complains about being treated like a princess, wearing a sparkling new tiara and a dress to die for, invited to attend lavish cocktail p—"

"—forced to attend," Finley would correct, before simmering in a corner, hoping to be left alone.

"Why do you have to be so ungrateful?" would be Eleanor's parting shot.

Finley would endeavour to escape to some sort of sanctuary to survive those dull weekends, usually the stables. Ernest would find her discussing equine-related subjects with her host's stable lads, stunned by her sudden angelic appearance.

Finley had no airs about her. She was happiest in the company of 'normal people', not 'toffs'. They were straightforward, and so was she. She was a natural around horses. The workers were always impressed by her knowledge and skill and wondered how she might have acquired it.

Lester had overheard a young aristocrat complain, 'I have met her once or twice, but she is not fit for marriage. She has a formidable character. In fact, she is downright terrifying. I have seen her ride like a man, shoot like a man. She is likely to fight like a man as well. She is usually accompanied by a clan of unruly brothers who idolise her. It would be as if I were marrying Boudica and her army.'

Finley hoped her father would put an end to this silly charade sooner rather than later, but he had a much bigger battle on his hands. One from which he was unlikely to return. If only the girl knew what peril her father was in, she would have had much bigger problems to consider.

3

THE BATTLE BALACLAVA

Harrington might be a cavalry officer, but he didn't choose his career. It chose him. His father was a military man, and he felt he had no option but to follow in his father's footsteps. After years of degradation, it was Ernest's last attempt to win his father's respect. Alas, it made no difference to Clement Harrington if his son was a general or a coal miner—he didn't love him.

Ernest's enthusiasm for war soured as he aged. Where he had always been a fearless warrior on the battlefield, the memories of his wife and children at home haunted him as he stormed toward the enemy. Nothing could elevate him more than returning to home comforts after experiencing the horror of fighting. Every time he shoved his bayonet into a young man, he would think of his eldest son, Lester, and it became more difficult to be an effective soldier. As an experienced combat soldier, he knew any delayed reaction could cost him his life.

It was not his courage that failed him. It was the futility of it all. As a young man, it was an honour to fight for Her Majesty. The army lured boys, not men. They were hardly beyond their childhood years when they joined up. Old soldiers no longer revered honour and bravery. It was not sufficient motivation to do their jobs. Their psyches were damaged by the continuous exposure to the images of death, suffering, disease, and starvation. Every night when they lay down to sleep, scenes of hell incarnate came alive in their minds, and the demons of war bombarded their souls.

*

Canon fire burst all around him when Harrington was thrown from his horse. He flew through the air and landed face down in mud and animal excrement. Looking up, he watched as horses' hooves missed crushing his skull within only a few inches. His own stallion lay a few yards away with its front leg broken. The animal was panicked and trying to get up, but its eyes rolled in their sockets in horror and pain. Ernest felt nauseous as he saw the limb bent so awkwardly out of place.

"Shoot it, damn you," he shouted to a nearby infantryman. "Shoot!"

The young man turned to look at the beast, the muzzle of his rifle trembling close to the beast's lolling head. There was a loud crack as the bullet was unleashed, then a sickening thud as the animal slumped to the ground.

1854 had been a brutal year for the British Army. Colonel Harrington lay on a battlefield amidst a carnage that he had never witnessed before. There was an ominous lull in the battle, and the scene around him was one of total devastation. The Light Cavalry Regiment were the bravest of men he had ever commanded, but the fatalities of the current campaign were the highest of any individual battle that he had ever fought.

*

A smoky cloud hung over the valley, and the smell of gunpowder saturated the air. The Battle of Balaclava was a slaughter, with the blood of friend, foe, and animal seeping into the earth.

He could see Lord Raglan at a distance, holding a telescope to his eye and looking down upon the hell that he had orchestrated in the valley. Ernest glared at the man who had sent his men to their death. Raglan had never commanded a battle before. His inexperience had resulted in this disaster. The man deserved to be court-martialled and hanged. That wouldn't happen. Raglan would claim victory, measured in the miles of territory he had conquered. If success was measured in deaths, he would have failed.

Harrington knew that he must get up and supervise the care of the men around him. He needed a rifle and bayonet, so he wrestled one from the hands of a dead man who stared up at him with vacant eyes. *'This is my last war. I want to go home.'*

*

Young William Russell, a war correspondent for The Times, had a clear view of the battlefield. Helpless, he watched the British High Command mistaking the enemy's position, sending their soldiers into the firing lines of the cannons that belched out smoke from the hill crest above. Men began to fall like a scythe rips through a wheatfield.

Until then, Russell's only experience of war was what he had read. The reality sickened him.

There was a lull in the fighting, and the men were relieved that they had driven back the enemy, oblivious to the Russian stragglers at the periphery. The British troops tried to rally themselves. Russell pondered that the fighting was over—but as fast as the thought came to mind, his wish was denied.

The young journalist watched as remnants of the Russian cavalry charged down the hill in a desperate effort to prove their honour. A bugle sounded a warning. They reached the battlefield in a renewed attack against the Light Brigade. Their gunners began to fire upon the scene below them. It was mayhem.

His report said that it was the most despicable act of betrayal he had ever witnessed. The Russian Army mowed down everyone on the battlefield, including their own men. The entire event had taken twenty minutes.

*

It took a dazed Colonel Harrington a moment to realise that the enemy had renewed their attack. He crawled and sheltered behind his dead horse. Red-hot grapeshot rained down, and his fate would depend upon where it fell. Ernest felt burning fire rip into his chest. Pain drilled through his kneecap, pinning him in position. Warm blood soaked into his tunic.

So excruciating was the pain, he would have sold his soul to the devil to stop it. The agony screeched through his brain until he could take it no more. Gasping, he pressed his hands on his wounds, gritting his teeth until his jaw muscles gave out. The light began to recede as the blood loss worsened.

*

William Russell made for the harbour at full gallop. He needed to dispatch the news immediately. Everyone at home would be waiting for it. He wrapped his report in an oilskin, put it into a leather bag, then wound layers of string around the parcel. Finally, he sealed the knot with wax and pushed his stamp into the molten red liquid. *'My words must not be corrupted.'*

"Thanks again," he muttered.

The harbourmaster dipped his pen in the inkwell as William watched the nib scratch out the words on the address label.

Mr JT Delane, Editor
The Times, London

The manuscript began its journey with a courier on horseback, then onto a cart. It crossed the Black Sea by ship until it reached Bucharest, where it was sent via telegraph to London.

The article would be published two weeks later, and no matter how unpopular it was with the government or whatever public outrage it would create, John Delane was determined to publish the truth about the death and destruction that had stalked the brave British forces on that blood-soaked battlefield.

4

THE NEWS

It was warm, and the sun shone gloriously, unusual weather for early autumn. The Harrington siblings were sitting in the dining room waiting for the first meal of the day. The only thing that spoilt the morning was the absence of their father. His seat at the head of the table was empty.

Mr Pearce, the butler, opened the magnificent mahogany doors and strode into the room, carrying the daily newspaper, collected from the village and carefully ironed.

Finley jumped to her feet and held out her hand with a smile.

"Thank you, Mr Pearce."

The valet looked at Finley fondly. He had known the girl from childhood, and now she was a beautiful young woman. Of all five children, she was his favourite, probably because she was so cheerful and spirited.

Reading the headlines was a daily ritual in the household of late, and everyone at the table held their breath, anxious to hear if there was any news about the war. Everyone that is, except for Eleanor. Finley put The Times on the table, unfurling it until the broadsheet covered all the place settings.

"That newspaper will render our pristine tablecloth pitch black, Finley. Put that rag away. I don't appreciate your despicable habit of reading at the table," chastised her stepmother.

Finley ignored the dreadful woman, far too engrossed in what she was doing to pay attention, let alone respond.

*

From the moment that Eleanor arrived at the farmhouse, she had set about making the girl miserable. She didn't anticipate that she would come up against the joint forces of Finley, Miss Reeves, and the Harrington boys. All attempts at being the 'Lady of the Manor' failed. Her stepchildren were too old to be controlled.

Eleanor Harrington might have charmed her husband into believing that she could be a benevolent force in his children's lives, but in truth, she was a conniving gold digger.

She had put a lot of thought into finding a husband. With no desire to have children, the man in question would have to be much older. Eleanor was determined that she would have some social stature and a foot in the door of London society. She had languished in relative obscurity for far too long. She decided to draw her prey to her, much like beautiful siren nymphs lured unsuspecting sailors onto the rocks.

When the colonel promptly proposed and whisked her off to a registry office, she was delighted. She almost cried when she reached her new home, such was the disappointment. There was nothing stately about the place at all. It was a tumble-down Tudor farmhouse, with a scraggy-looking thatched roof, surrounded by fields filled with grazing cows. The arable landscape had clearly not had Capability

Brown's critical eye cast upon it, nor could the property boast an elaborate driveway, which was a 'must' for receiving guests. The flagstone floors were covered by worn carpets. The furniture was old and functional. The servants were unsophisticated country folk who didn't wear uniforms. Those and many more irritations drove the message home. Eleanor Jeffreys had backed the wrong horse.

When she told her husband that she needed money to improve her standard of living, Ernest Harrington told her that it could wait, advising her he was settling the hefty debts that had accrued during the lean years.

This financial bombshell was the end of their relationship, even when the family's fortunes returned to full health. Eleanor moved into her own bedroom and stayed there, hiding the decision behind the lie of Ernest needing his rest when he came home. The one positive to come out of the disastrous marriage was that her husband's good name and military title did gain her access to the rich.

*

Finley looked at William Russell's war correspondence. The brothers waited in anticipation for her to read the first sentences as normal.

They watched their sister's eyes move across the words, then jumped when she sat bolt upright, her face registering a combination of shock and surprise.

"What is it, Fin?" asked Lester.

Finley cleared her throat, desperate for her voice not to sound croaky with emotion, as she read aloud.

"Victorious British suffer huge losses at Battle of Balaclava!"

"Impossible," Lester blurted out. "Which regiment? Out with it."

"The cavalry. The Light Brigade. One of the regiments that father commanded."

Lester stood up and snatched at the newspaper and began to read.

"We shall discuss this matter in the parlour, not over the breakfast table," said their stepmother, raising her voice in annoyance in the break in protocol.

"This is terrible news," said Finley, looking over Lester's shoulder.

"How dare you disobey me!" demanded Eleanor, who was struggling to maintain her feigned upper-class composure.

"Please don't interrupt," said Lester sternly. "Can't you see we are concerned about our father?"

"Will the War Office give you information on papa, Lester? Surely they'll tell you?"

"I don't know, Fin. I doubt it. Britain has every ship in the fleet sitting in the Black Sea. It's a catastrophe. The whole campaign's been a dismal diplomatic and military failure. The government is bound to want to hush things up. It's what governments always do in the face of a public outcry."

"I doubt that they will have information for us in particular. More than half the brigade is dead, dying or missing," Edward muttered in disbelief. "It must be chaos out there."

"But we have to find papa! We must!" said Finley, banging her fists on the table, jangling the crockery.

For once, her brothers didn't pay any attention.

"What irony. We have lost so many troops in this battle, and the generals had the gall to call it a victory yesterday. If it was not for this article by Mr Russell, we would never have realised the truth!"

"It sounds like a slaughter," whispered Lester, his heart thumping in his chest like a navy's pickaxe on rock.

Finley was determined to be heard.

"We must find out if Papa is still alive, Lester. You must find somebody who can help us."

"Stop it at once, Finley," Eleanor Harrington interrupted. "You are upsetting me. We are entering the Christmas season, and all this talk of war is spoiling everything. Besides, it is unbecoming for a young lady of your status to be involved in discussions of war and politics."

"Upsetting you? What about us?" the girl yelled. "Our government sacrifices people like my father—your husband—at their every whim and the soldiers are paid a meagre stipend for their trouble. Are you not concerned?"

Eleanor, as always, was more concerned about her husband's will than his wellbeing. For her, this was playing out rather nicely. She glared, expecting the siblings to capitulate.

"Our queen is a plundering savage like all the other monarchs of Europe. Nothing has changed in a thousand years," added the youngest son, Clive

"Those are treacherous words! How dare you? If you continue with your outrageous and outspoken opinions, you may find yourselves at the end of a rope," said Eleanor venomously, secretly wishing it would happen.

"We should have emigrated to Australia and bought a sheep farm like papa suggested," Lester muttered, regretting not supporting the idea more when it was first mooted.

"A farm in Australia?" Eleanor screeched, finally coming to the end of her tether.

"That's right," answered Clive, "a calm, peaceful life down under."

"We are not convicts. Over my dead body. Those common people are thoroughly offensive."

Eleanor trembled with so much anger her hair was escaping from its disciplined arrangement, giving her an air of someone quite demented.

"I am not so sure about that anymore, Eleanor. Our own nation, committing frightful atrocities across the globe to satisfy the greed of wealthy men," Clive added with a frown.

"We need raw materials to support the war effort. You can't run campaigns on fresh air." Eleanor countered.

"There would be no wars if our country traded instead of conquered."

"Why is no one talking about finding Papa!" Finley blurted out, her gaze demanding an answer but not getting one.

"How dare you, Clive! You have a duty to honour the British Empire."

"We do support the Empire, Eleanor," interrupted Lester, trying to subdue the situation, "but our government is not making wise decisions for its people. Papa agrees. He watches good men die every day fighting in these foreign places. It's not right."

Eleanor threw her cutlery down with a clang as metal met porcelain and threw her napkin across the table.

"How else would we rid ourselves of the dreaded underclasses if they are not used as cannon fodder?" Eleanor mumbled snidely.

"Well, stepmother, if they are still alive, you could employ them to wipe your privileged arse."

Everyone looked at Finley aghast. Later Lester and Clive would laugh about it, but in the moment, they were shocked. Mr Pearce left the room in a hurry, lest he burst into gales of laughter. That comment would make for some entertaining gossip in the kitchen. Eleanor's anger boiled over.

"You are an embarrassment to this family, Finley Harrington. A disgrace. You will never find a husband. I am ashamed to tell people that I am even related to you,"

"Modern women are not looking for a husband. They want an education and to vote."

"Stop it with your mindless drivel. You'll never reach a university, let alone a ballot box," Eleanor sneered.

Lester interrupted the argument.

"Our father has raised us to create our own destiny, and we shall go about it as we wish. Finley will marry for love and happiness, not selfishly—not for money, prestige or to further her station in society."

Eleanor knew that the last words were a direct criticism of her marriage motives. It was the final blow of the miserable morning for her, convinced that she would have a stroke if she didn't get out of the breakfast room. She held not an ounce of affection for her twenty-one-year-old stepdaughter and longed to be rid of the problems she caused.

As Eleanor pursed her lips, she wished she could banish Finley from the house—or at least put her into a convent somewhere far away—but those were fantasies. When she had suggested that the 'wayward girl' attend an elite boarding school for young ladies, Ernest had told her to never broach the subject again, and it was clear it was not another argument over money.

The shrew was jealous of the love that her husband showered upon his children. Ernest was unlike other men in that respect. She never realised that he would have been just as dedicated to his marriage if she had stayed loyal to him.

When it came to Eleanor's relationship with Finley, jealousy turned to envy, envy to hate, as the current Mrs Harrington strove to be the most beautiful, most powerful woman in the household. After the heated argument over breakfast, both women were even more determined to trounce their rival.

5

THE GENERAL

Finley and her four brothers sat in the library, its walls lined with shelves carrying literature from all over the globe. A haven for their father when he was at home, he found solace and inspiration in the place. It renewed his faith in mankind.

That troubling morning, there was none of the carefree banter that usually accompanied a reunion, and the place was even quieter without him.

"There is still no specific information for us," Lester informed the others. "There are simply too many dead and wounded to deal with. The War Office's administrative unit has been besieged by hundreds of people demanding news of their loved ones. It was bedlam when I visited last time. I thought a riot would ensue. The authorities assured us that they will distribute information as soon as they receive word from Constantinople."

"And the army? Surely father's unit must have some idea?" moaned Clive.

"Not a clue," Lester said. "I thought I would try a little military campaign of my own. I visited many of my father's close friends, the high-ranking ones. Nothing."

"How can it be that this man, Mr Russell, a civilian who works for The Times, can provide information so rapidly?" Finley protested but to no avail.

"What do you suggest we do?" asked the second eldest son, John.

"The true situation remains elusive," said Edward. "The good news is our company will soon lay a sub-marine cable that will improve communications in the Black Sea and across the Mediterranean."

"Rolls of wire stacked in the dockyard aren't much use, are they? What about papa!" Finley muttered.

"Newall & Co. had no success convincing the government or the military that modern communications are crucial to winning wars. Lord Raglan has been negative. Says it's unnecessary," Edward explained.

"He is terrified that the news of his inept command will reach us faster, more like," mumbled Clive.

"Perhaps that's why it has taken private industrialists to fund this engineering project, not the government, Clive."

"I believe that Hudson's Forge in Birmingham has played a significant role in the design of the cable delivery mechanism."

"Oh yes, John. Samuel is a brilliant engineer. Not afraid to roll his sleeves up either. He and his men are loading a ship with spindles as we speak," said Edward. "It is quite mind-boggling. Can you believe that each spindle has twelve-and-a-half miles of cable wound onto it?"

John gazed outside. Beneath a grimy grey sky, swaying trees yielded their leaves to the ravages of a brisk northerly wind. The young man's thoughts turned to winter.

"The weather in Crimea is treacherous at this time of year. I take some comfort knowing money is pouring in from all over the country to support our brave men."

"Russell says that the hospital facilities are a disgrace," said Finley. "What if father is recuperating there?"

The siblings' faces fell silent until a gloomy John continued their discussion.

"The frozen earth is bound to hamper us laying those cables."

"The government is using every private vessel available to transport goods, food and ammunition to the Black Sea," said John.

"So, what can we do?" insisted Edward.

Finley stared at the bleak newspaper headline, stomach tightening, jaw clenched, breathing deep.

"We need information upon which we can act. I will contact Mr Russell. Perhaps he has access to better information than we are receiving from the army. Perhaps if father is wounded, we can arrange his repatriation using the cable supply ships?"

"Perhaps? Lester? This is our father's survival we are talking about," tutted Clive. "Time is of the essence! We should leave as soon as possible. We must be able to do something."

Edward rose to his feet:

"We have to!"

"It's not that simple—it's a blasted war zone! Act in haste, repent at leisure."

As the brothers' frustration grew, stalling them sounded cowardly and redundant, but Lester refused to risk the impetuous fellows' lives. At the same time, he had to force himself to follow his own advice. *'Father would agree with my decision. I must be firm with them. We can't let our heads be ruled by our hearts.'*

Finley, never troubled by such trivial rules, sat reading the article again, pouring over every detail.

*

Mr Pearce got quite a fright from the thunderous sound of the cold brass knocker against the front door. He had no idea who was calling, but it sounded official. On the doorstep was a military figure, decorated with so many medals that he would have been weighed down if it weren't for his large stature. General Anthony Logan and his aide-de-camp stood on the front step, oozing authority.

Pearce wondered what warranted a visit from such important men. The answer was simple. They were there to announce the death of Colonel Harrington.

"Good morning, gentlemen."

"Mrs Harrington," the aide commanded rudely.

"I beg your pardon?" Pearce said, feigning ignorance.

The butler had a way of making life difficult for discourteous people, and he liked to use it liberally.

"General Logan and I are here to see Mrs Harrington."

"Will you follow me, please, gentlemen?"

The silvery-haired general looked Pearce in the eye and gave a slight nod.

"As you wish," said the aide.

Pearce showed the guests to the parlour. Hearing the footsteps, Lester peered around the library door and spotted the glint of brass buttons on the cuffs of the khaki uniforms. With ears angled towards the doors, the others eavesdropped.

"Please wait here. I shall fetch Mrs Harrington forthwith, General."

With thumping hearts, the siblings marched to the parlour in double-quick time.

*

Lester Harrington shook General Logan's hand and introduced him to the others.

"And this is my sister, Miss Finley Harrington."

The general shook her hand and held it too firmly and too long. *'My, my! Ernest Harrington has bred a beautiful daughter. I wonder if she's susceptible to the charms of an older man of means and status.'*

Finley pulled her hand away roughly, instinctively realising the general's intentions from his lecherous stare and dominating persona. She was delighted when her stepmother arrived, eager to charm the important man.

"Good morning, General Logan," said Eleanor as she breezed into the parlour, perfectly coiffed and powdered.

"Mrs Harrington," answered the general.

He had always considered the woman a beauty, but she paled in comparison to her stepdaughter.

"You have business to discuss?" Eleanor cooed charmingly. "The young Harringtons were just preparing to leave the room."

A face like thunder, she glared at them.

"Perhaps they should remain here. I am afraid my news is grave."

Eleanor pouted at being denied a private audience. Finley moved closer to Lester, and he gripped her hand. The eldest was convinced that their father was dead and was already planning how to shield his siblings from the terrible blow.

Finley had already decided that her father was alive but in danger.

"I don't want to seem impolite, but what I wish to discuss is perhaps too distressing for Miss Harrington to hear. Can she be escorted from the room?"

"I agree, general," said Eleanor, giving Finley a small dismissive nod.

Already getting a sense of the girl's precocious determination, General Logan nodded at his aide, who took a few steps toward Finley, intending to take her arm and forcibly escort her from the library. Dreamy Clive, who normally lived in his own little world, darted in front of the aide.

"Miss Harrington will stay in the room," Lester added with conviction.

"General Logan has ordered her to leave the room. It is not an instruction," the aide snapped.

It was as if the family were soldiers on the parade square.

"This is not the army, sir. This is a private home. By proxy, Lester Harrington is the head of this house until my father returns," Clive boomed.

The aide flushed bright red. General Logan turned around and looked at Finley and then at Clive. He was not used to having his orders questioned, and he found it difficult to maintain his temper.

"Very well," said General Logan sarcastically. "I shall continue. Let us hope that Miss Harrington does not suffer a breakdown."

It was Finley's turn to struggle—to contain her contempt. *'How dare he write me off like that! The cheek of the fellow.'*

"What news do you have for us today, general?" Eleanor twittered, secretly wishing her husband's fate would lead to her freedom.

"We only have little information about Colonel Harrington. As you know, it takes some time for news to arrive in London."

"Perhaps you should consult the editor of the Times," chided Finley. "They seem more equipped at disseminating information than Her Majesty's army."

The general began to understand that the Harringtons were nothing like the other families he had met before. They were fierce, educated, unfettered by the rules of etiquette and protocol. *'Since when did anyone criticise Her Majesty's forces?'*

"We believe that your father has been captured by the Russian Army. We don't know if he is dead or alive. Lord Raglan has told me that he can't do anything more until the spring as a terrible hurricane struck the Black Sea. A large part of the allied fleet has been lost."

"In the spring?" asked Finley. "That's months away!"

Her gut scrunched tighter still. She worked her hand loose from Lester's in case her grip crushed his palm to a pulp.

"Is he behind enemy lines, General?" asked John.

"We don't know. All we have is a witness statement that he was seen being dragged off the battlefield by a Russian soldier."

"General, how long before he is presumed dead?" asked Eleanor.

The siblings were stunned by her open show of appalling self-interest. A new low had been breached.

"It will be six months until the official announcement that he is deceased, Mrs Harrington. Then, you can make arrangements for probate."

"This is a terrible blow to all of us, of course. But thankfully, Ernest was a pragmatic man, and he has provided well for this eventuality."

Even by Eleanor's standards, this comment was mercenary.

"How many men are missing at the moment?" asked Edward

"We simply don't know," answered General Logan.

"Surely Raglan can count?" interrupted Finley. "Are you telling me he's even more incompetent than I presumed?"

"A man of your father's rank is at an elevated risk of being captured and tortured for information," the aide added cruelly as he looked at Finley, hoping to incite hysterics.

Keen to take on the mantle of grieving widow, Eleanor whispered, 'I do hope my husband has the constitution to survive such brutality,' but fooled no one with her empty words.

The Harrington children began demanding answers from him thick and fast, the general became enraged.

"I don't trust Lord Raglan's judgement," Finley prodded again.

General Logan tried to ignore her but failed to keep his composure.

"I don't think we need the opinion of a woman in this discussion, Miss Harrington. War belongs in the realm of men's responsibility. With all due respect, my dear, I know you mean well. But you couldn't possibly understand."

It was frustrating enough that he had to suffer Miss Nightingale in the last months. The woman had been deeply critical of him, highlighting his indifference for the men under his command. She had even questioned his commitment as a leader because his men lay starving and diseased. It might have been her first taste of the brutality of warfare, but it wasn't his.

"You underestimate me. General Logan. As an educated, well-read daughter of a colonel, I understand the intricacies of this campaign all too well. We wouldn't be in this abominable situation if it were not for Raglan. Which buffoon appointed him to lead an army? This the greatest blunder in the history of the British military."

General Logan's voice changed from one of authority to one of command.

"Please tell Miss Harrington to leave the room immediately," General Logan ordered Lester. "She is obviously distressed."

"I don't give my sister orders, sir. If you wish to tell her something, you are welcome to do it yourself."

The man turned to face Finley. Anybody else would have been intimidated by his crisp starched uniform, gold braid and mass of medals. His black boots shone like a mirror. Now his voice was deep and booming.

"Miss Harrington, I order you to leave the room."

"Oh, General Logan, thank you for taking control of the situation," Eleanor piped up. "I am embarrassed by my stepdaughter's outburst. Please accept my apology for her lack of manners."

But the two military men were fools to underestimate Finley's significance, motherless so young, growing up in a family of men. With an officer father, she would never be intimidated by a mere uniform. It was who wore it that would earn her respect.

"General Logan, I have been raised as an equal to my brothers. Do not give me orders in this house. Thankfully, I am not a soldier on your battlefield. Have you forgotten your place, Sir? You work at the behest of the nation, a servant protecting our country."

"Silence!" boomed Logan.

"You will allow me to continue, sir," she said calmly. "If Lord Raglan can't find my father, I will show him how to."

The general's face went blood red. 'If she had been a man under my command, she would have had her beaten for insubordination—as close to death as was legally possible. If I ever meet this creature alone, I will make her pay for her insolence in a manner that will satisfy my desires and dominating tendencies.'

"We have a good grasp of the situation," said Lester "thank you for calling on us."

A furious Logan knew that he was being dismissed. No Harrington would ever be accepted into the army again. 'I'll make sure that their father never receives another validation for his bravery—alive or dead.' But the general's wishes didn't matter. Ernest wanted none of his offspring to enter the military. Besides, his sons wanted to build, not destroy.

The general marched out of the room in a dreadful temper. Eleanor Harrington followed on his heels, close to tears. *Those ungrateful brats are ruining any opportunity I have for a proper future.'*

"General, General," Eleanor called after him. "Won't you please join me for tea before you leave?"

Logan had no idea why she had ever married Ernest Harrington. Such a beauty deserved to be treated to a more refined, regal lifestyle—not the circus that she lived in. Out in the corridor, she turned to her, gently taking her hand.

"Perhaps another time, my dear," he said charmingly. "I will find any food or drink unpalatable after my experience of your stepdaughter."

"Finley is incorrigible. I have told Ernest that she'll cast a shadow upon this family," Eleanor whispered.

"Don't apologise for her, my dear. You can't be held responsible for the girl's character."

"I hope I am not speaking out of turn, general, but I believe I read in the paper you became a widower some months ago. I am so sorry for your loss." Eleanor cooed sympathetically.

"It was a great shock when my beloved wife passed. Recently, I have forced myself to become more social. I have been invited to Lord Paxton's country house in Surrey. If you happen to receive an invitation, I will be delighted to share my experience over a cup of tea, or perhaps something stronger."

Eleanor, thrilled, tensed her face to fight off the threat of a broad grin. A thin smile graced her angelic face instead. The handsome soldier had as good as proposed they meet privately. *'What luck!'*

General Logan, suddenly remembering he was supposed to be marched to the front door and stood before it, waiting for Mr Pearce to open it, but the old butler was missing.

Pearce had charged to the kitchen to give the staff a first-hand account of Finley's rebellion, which delighted them.

The general's aide-de-camp was forced to open the door for the two of them himself. It was a great social insult, and it didn't go unnoticed.

6

THE PLAN

It was snowing, but not the gentle flakes that drifted down like powder. It was the kind driven by gale force winds and slanted as it fell. Out of the window, the land looked as smooth and white as an iced wedding cake.

Finley had not slept at all, spending the night pacing up and down her room. Late in the evening, she and Lester had tussled over the question of her father.

"We must wait for more information, Finley. How can we come up with a plan with so few facts? In the face of such danger?"

"The only news we have of our father is that he has been captured by Russian forces. Else he may be dead or dying in some disease-infested casualty clearing station. I don't see how waiting will help with his situation so perilous. The closer we get to his location, the more information we will have. We shall learn on the way."

"Have you lost your mind, Finley?"

"No. It is here, as determined and focused as ever," she hissed, jabbing at her temple.

Her brother gave a long sigh, cheeks puffed out, lips pursed. He glanced up at the ornate library ceiling, waiting for his frustration to simmer down.

"Alright. Have it your way, Lester. Let's sleep on it. See how we feel in a day or two? Then decide?"

Wishing she would drop the line of relentless questioning, Lester chose to lie.

"An excellent suggestion. With rested heads, we'll be far more objective. Until tomorrow then?" he said as he made his way to the door.

The more she pondered the situation, the more she was convinced immediate action was the only sensible option. *'Father is lying in some godforsaken country, sick, wounded or being tortured is unbearable. I could never live with myself knowing that I made no effort to save him.'* She put her hands on the icy cold windowpane, looking out on the blizzard. *'Goodness knows how cold the Crimea is! My brothers can wait until they have reams of information, but I should leave immediately. There isn't time the be paralysed with indecision.'*

Finley believed that if she tried hard enough, she could overcome any problem. She thought back to the national sensation, Grace Darling. A lighthouse keeper's daughter, she braved a terrible storm to rescue nine survivors of a shipwrecked on the rocky Northumbrian shoreline. *'Did she sit on land fretting? Waiting for a man to give her permission to act. No, she did not!'*

This was no different to any other challenge she had faced before. Only the scale had changed. True, the journey would be uncomfortable. But it was only a journey, not some sort of epic, ancient Greek saga. *'My father has experienced many difficult conditions and desperate situations. But if he was able to live through them, so can I. I am Colonel Ernest Harrington's daughter after all.'*

Over the past year, Finley had keenly followed the newspaper articles about Florence Nightingale, another woman who made herself unpopular in the name of righteousness. The tenacious woman's bravery inspired Finley, and the more she read, the braver she became. Every detail of her endeavours was etched in the young girl's mind. Her travels and results were well-documented, especially by those who wanted to see the woman be toppled from her perch. Finley, on the other hand, wished her nothing but success.

On Florence's arrival in Scutari with a complement of over two hundred nurses, Miss Nightingale was appalled by the filth and neglect the soldiers were suffering. Medicine was in short supply. Basic hygiene was neglected. Mass infections, many of which were fatal, were far frequent. Even basic equipment to prepare food for the patients was sorely lacking. Publicly berating the government in The Times, Florence ensured the authorities were forced to capitulate and commission Brunel to create a prefabricated hospital that could be built in England and brought to the Dardanelles. It was there, at this new civilian-run hospital, that Nightingale had reduced the fatality rate to less than one-tenth of the military hospital in Scutari.

Reading about Florence's gumption, plus the frequent calls for women to take up nursing posts in the papers had opened Finley's mind to a wealth of possibilities that has passed her busy brothers by. Many men might be happy to write off the fairer sex, but young Miss Harrington was not inclined to climb into their prison-like pigeon-hole.

The plan for her next step was abruptly interrupted by a knock on the door. Having seen the light leak out from the surround, Lester knew the answer to his question but whispered through the keyhole anyway.

"Fin? Are you awake? I need to talk to you."

"Come in. What has happened?" Is it father?" Finley asked, expecting the worst.

"No," said Lester. "In all the brouhaha, I forgot to tell you I need to travel to Southampton soon. They are putting tons of ammunition onto the ships, and the Home Office is concerned about the safety at the docks. They have asked my employer to oversee the loading. They believe that the men are exhausted, so the shifts must be managed correctly, or they could blow Southampton sky high."

Lester gave a nervous laugh, and his sister reciprocated. It was the first time they had laughed together all day.

"When are you off?"

"When I said, 'soon', I really meant I leave for Southampton tomorrow morning. The last thing I want to do is leave you alone. This is a challenging time for you. For all of us. Of course, I know you will be fine. Your brothers will look after you, but still, I would prefer to be here."

"It's not your fault," she reassured. "How long will you be gone for?

"A fortnight, give or take."

He frowned, his hands writhing together in his lap.

"—I don't know how you're going to manage with Eleanor."

"That harpy? Fear not. She's no match for me, Lester."

Her glowing grin shone brighter than the lamp light.

"I don't think papa loves her anymore," Finley confessed. "He knows that she's a selfish shrew. I am certain he married her so we could have a loving mother—and she has failed dismally. Now, he is just a means to an end for her. Her glee at the news he might be dead? Well, that was the last straw for me. I refuse to even be civil."

Lester nodded, pensive, brooding. She looked at her big brother as she held his hands still. He had always been a shoulder she could cry on, albeit seldom.

"Who is this Hudson man you were discussing yesterday?" She asked Lester.

"A good chap, by all accounts. Only met him in passing. Self-made man. Owns premises in Birmingham. He flits between Birmingham and London's Mayfair."

Without knowing it, Lester's interruption had helped Finley to formulate her plan.

In the morning, she sent one of the stable lads on the train to London on a reconnaissance expedition. On his return, she asked him to take her to the Mayfair address she had been looking for.

*

Arriving at Samuel Hudson's house, the wintery gale buffeted her on the walk from the coach to the door. It stung her reddened face. Her dress acted like a sail as the severe gusts pushed her about.

The door was opened by a cheerful young man, who didn't bother to greet her.

> "Come, come. Miss! Quickly now. You will be frozen solid if you don't get out of this beastly weather."

> "I must apologise for arriving unannounced, but this is an urgent matter. I am the daughter of Colonel Ern—

Before she could state her business, Finley heard a booming voice from somewhere within the townhouse.

> "Who is at the door, Socrates? I told you that I don't want visitors today."

> "It is a young lady to see us, Mr Samuel," shouted the servant.

It was an unusual exchange between master and servant. Finley was fascinated.

> "Alone?"

> "Yes, Sam."

"Where is she? Bring her through to my study, please."

A little girl appeared from behind Socrates, black-haired with spectacular green eyes. Even at this early age, Finley could see that she would make a beautiful woman.

"Don't be afraid, Miss," the child advised. "Papa makes a dreadful noise, but he is really very kind."

Finley smiled. She was enjoying the lack of formality already.

"If you want my advice, follow the girl," said Socrates with a smile. "She has her father wrapped around her little finger, and he can never be angry when he sees her."

"Then I am in safe hands," Finley chuckled as she bent down to give the girl a handshake.

Shilling led the curious visitor into Samuel Hudson's study.

"Look, Papa! I have brought a guest, and she has hair the same colour as Miss Annabelle."

Samuel looked at the child and smiled. His eyes were gentle. He gave a deep laugh that forced Finley to smile as well.

"Indeed, it is," the industrialist agreed. "It is very lovely."

"Is Miss Anabelle your dolly?" Finley smiled.

"No, ma'am. She looks after me like a mother. My mother d—"

"That's enough from you, I think, young lady. You are telling Miss Harrington all our business," Samuel chortled. "Now off you go. Find Socrates and ask Cook to give you a piece of cake."

Samuel Hudson watched the child leave before he greeted Finley. Breaking the rules yet again, she put out her hand to introduce herself. Her directness impressed Samuel.

"Mr Hudson—"

"Please, call me Sam."

"—Sam. My name is Miss Finley Harrington, daughter of Colonel Ernest Harrington."

Samuel studied her for a moment. She was an attractive woman, brimming with confidence. Taking that to be a good sign, he extended his hand to hers.

Finley was taken with Samuel from the moment that they met. She had never met a man so comfortable with himself, or with her, apart from Lester perhaps. It was refreshing to meet such a confident, unstuffy man. She knew that they were going to be friends. He offered her tea, which she politely declined, eager to get down to the real purpose of her visit.

"Apparently, you know my brother Edward Harrington," said Finley.

"Indeed, I do," smiled Samuel, curious to discover the reason for her visit as well.

"Edward mentioned that you are currently loading reels of cable onto a steamer moored near Millwall."

Samuel nodded, impressed.

"I am looking for a passage to the Black Sea."

"Why do you want to go there?" asked Samuel. matter of fact.

"I'd rather not say. I am afraid that you will tell my brothers," Finley answered honestly.

"Are you suggesting I am a gossip, Miss Harrington?"

"No! No!"

Samuel sat back in his chair with his arms behind his head and stared at her without saying another word. She noted his hair was dishevelled, and his sleeves were bunched up around the elbows. The silence made her uncomfortable, unable to decide if divulging her secret would make matters better or worse.

"I hear that you can outride any man in the hunt," said Samuel, as a smile touched his lips.

Relief flooded a nodding Finley.

"—And you have a fine reputation with a rifle."

Finley didn't know where his statements were leading. The man seemed cordial, but was he? Samuel's directness would put her out of her misery.

"If you want my help, Finley, you need to tell me your intentions, or I can't give you sound advice."

"I am sorry, Mr Hu—"

"Sam."

"I am embarrassed. I should have known better than to withhold the facts. That is not a reflection of my true character, but I don't know if I can trust you yet."

"I have heard that you prefer to be frank," Sam teased. "So, let us start at the beginning—with the truth, shall we?"

Finley told him her story, and he listened carefully.

"So, in a nutshell—can you help me to get a passage on the steamer that is delivering the cable to the Black Sea— please?"

"Unfortunately not," answered Samuel, without a pause.

"Because I am a woman?"

"I think you should know me better than that, Finley", he shot back. "I can't assist because I don't own the ship."

"Surely you have influence?"

"I do, but if I ask somebody for a favour, I owe them a favour. I don't do business that way."

Deflated but defiant, she stood up to leave. The meeting was a failure and a humiliation. Finley had two flaws, she didn't like hearing the word 'no', and she didn't like hearing the word 'no' from a man.

"Sit down, Finley," he said softly, but it had the same effect as thunder.

Finley reluctantly complied.

"I am not threatened by strong women, Finley. In fact, I promote them. Your loyalty is touching, and I hope that my daughter would rescue me under similar circumstances. I am a commoner, not the regular class that you socialise with. I see the world a little differently."

"Don't associate me with the elite."

"Then stop behaving like one, then."

"Can I please excuse myself? I would like to leave now."

"No, you may not," Samuel advised. "You have come here for help. You need help. And I may have a solution."

Finley could hardly believe what she was hearing. She'd annoyed the man, and yet he was still prepared to help her. She surmised it wasn't her charm or beauty that had stirred him, like so many men before—it was her directness. Samuel Hudson appeared to be one of the most honourable people she would ever meet, but he was not stupid. *'I'd better not put this relationship to the test again because he might not be as forgiving a second time.'*

"Here is the name of a small rust tub in the new harbour. It looks terrifying, but the old man is the finest captain with whom you will ever sail. Thomas Grainger is a rough diamond, but he can read the elements, and you will reach Calais safely. That's as much as I can do for now."

"Thank you," she said, head bowed.

Finley was sincere, and he knew it.

"When I return, I will tell my brother Edward that you helped me."

"You will do no such thing!"

Finley looked puzzled. Why not thank the man for his kind deed?

"No, this is between you and me. I don't want Edward to think that he needs to repay me."

'That makes sense.'

"I will send a telegram to one of my close friends who is in Paris. He will help you. If you can get to the Gare du Lyon by seven o'clock tomorrow night, he'll travel with you to Marseille. There is only one train a day, so he'll meet you at the platform. There he can find a vessel that will take you to Balaclava."

Finley wanted to throw her arms around Samuel in joy. She smiled from ear to ear.

"What is his name?" she asked.

"Gabriel. Gabriel Craddick."

"The writer?"

"Yes."

*

Back at the family home, Finley remained tight-lipped about her foray to London, vaguely referring to some shopping errands. She kept out of the way as she finalised her grand scheme.

Choosing to travel with as little luggage as possible, she didn't want to impede her progress, and she didn't need any setbacks. This wasn't a jolly holiday. It was a deadly mission to one of the most terrible theatres of war of all time.

The case looked full to bursting. There was no room for anything useful she might pick up along the way. She looked at the clothing she had chosen to take with her, holding each piece up, judging its practicality. Even the simplest garments assumed too much space. Anything offering a shred of warmth was far too bulky to pack. She decided to wear as much as possible and take nothing extra. A stream of abandoned clothes sailed through the air back towards their home in her wardrobe. She slammed the door up against the heap of fabric, then collapsed onto her bed, staring up at the canopy above.

The Crimean winter was vicious, and she needed enough insulation to remain warm in the worst circumstances. *'I shall take a thick coat. Preferably something fur-lined. With a large snug hood.'*

She fished about her rag-tag collection of garments for something genuinely useful. A new pile of clothes materialised on her bed as she muttered in a temper.

'How do men get away with such small suitcases?'

Of course! She clasped her face in her hands, annoyed at her naivety.

'You silly girl. The answer lay in the question. You must dress as a man.'

She sneaked into Clive's room, opened his wardrobe, and began rifling through his clothes. He was a good six inches taller than her but the smallest of all her brothers.

She chose a coat that almost reached her ankles, but that wouldn't matter for what she had in mind. Knowing that the overcoat alone couldn't keep her warm enough if she was at sea or stuck in the snow, she selected two suits and a pair of thick woolly jumpers. Her plan was to alternate the suits, partly to offer an immediate disguise if needed and partly to offer something warm and dry to change into.

She stuffed the clothes into the case and hastily made her exit.

The house was perfectly still. Eleanor had gone to London, so her bedroom was next. The woman had a walk-in dressing room, and extravagant clothing hung neatly categorised, a perfect reflection of her materialistic nature. There was a mass of boots and shoes, in a range of styles and colours, that she had never seen her stepmother wear.

Soon, Finley snapped out of her discontentment and returned to the important matter of rifling through the coats. *'Cashmere. Mohair. Silk. Blast. These are useless.'* The hangers clattered as her arm swept one unsuitable garment after another along its rail. Finally, she found the collection of fur coats sheathed in cotton to protect them from moths and mildew. *'Too big. Too thin. Too bulky.'*

After much searching, she found exactly what she had been looking for— a light, snug-fitting fur coat with a hood lined with downy wool. She slid it on, then wrestled Clive's oversized coat on top. It fitted. Just.

To protect her lower legs, she planned to wear her trusty riding boots. Every inch of her body would be covered against wind and weather. Finley had never seen Eleanor wear the fur and doubted that the woman would miss it.

Next, Finley tiptoed to Lester's room, fighting to remove the two coats as she walked. Her hands explored her brother's top bedside drawer. When her fingertips met a cosy soft scarf, she curled it up into a neat roll and added it to her cache of clothing. A pair of thick over-the-knee socks were liberated. When all Lester's hats fell over her nose, it was time to move on.

She drew a blank at Edward's closet but did find a bowler hat in John's bedroom. A fit perfectly, the hat stayed in place when she tucked her hair underneath it.

In the mirror, she gazed at her reflection, tilting her head from side to side to admire her disguise, then turned away before her inner-self could look her in the eye and talk her out of the bold move ahead.

Back in her bedroom room, with some careful packing, the clothing that she had chosen perfectly fitted into the small case. Every time footsteps went along the landing, she flinched. Thankfully, no one came to check on her.

The Harringtons' home was a large one, and nobody noticed Finley slip out into the night. Dressed in the greatcoat, a man's suit of clothes, and her hair was knotted under her hat, she scuttled off to the closest village and waited for the late train to London. Anyone who saw the shadowy figure striding down the lane would have mistaken her for a young man. Halfway down the platform, she brushed the dusting of snow off a lonely bench and took a seat. Each tick of the loud clock reminded her she was another second closer to finding her father. By Finley's own admission, things were off to an immaculate start.

'Let's hope it stays that way.'

7

THE CROSSING

Finley arrived in London and made her way to the new Millwall dock on London's Isle of Dogs. The city seemed to decay before her eyes as she headed toward the East End. The area was notoriously a miserable pit of poverty. Its decrepit old streets were awash with the homeless, some sitting around open fires, others wrapped in layers of rags to keep the cold at bay. Everyone had dull deep-set eyes, parched faces, and clear signs of starvation.

If Finley had been wearing a dress, she would have been subjected to lewd comments and proposals, but as a man, she was anonymous. She pulled her coat collar up high. Sailors and prostitutes filled the small pubs and inns, and the screeching sounds of violins and penny whistles assaulted the air. Finley heard people copulating in the alleys, protected by the early afternoon dark. The streets smelled of urine, faeces, smoke, and beer. The raw stench threatened to turn her stomach.

She reached the dock and systematically walked the jetties searching for 'The Mighty Bess' and Mr Hudson's contact, Captain Grainger. Finley had hidden money everywhere on her person. She had a few quid in her pockets. The rest was hidden in the folds of her socks, sewn into her hat, her trousers' waistbands, and the fur coat. She was glad that if a light-fingered little tyke pickpocketed her, there would be enough money hidden somewhere else on her person.

The cash needed to be squirrelled away since Finley had taken money to last six months. It was an exorbitant amount of money, but she was loathed to risk being stranded alone without any.

*

It wasn't that odd that Finley didn't take breakfast or luncheon that day. It wasn't the first time the feisty girl failed to appear on demand. However, when she was not there for afternoon tea, her brothers became concerned. No one recalled seeing her anywhere. By dinnertime, they were really fed up with her.

> "She could have left a note and told us where she had gone," complained Clive.

Frustration turned to resentment, then to worry. It was their churning guts that spurred the brothers into action.

> "She can't have gone far. I bet she's got herself in a tizzy with this argument about how to help papa, that's all. She'll cool down and come back," John said.

> "I bet she's gone to Mimi's," added Edward. "Let's give it a bit longer, eh? She'll go mad if she thinks we've been pacing about fussing."

Mimi was Finley's best friend, a like-minded bohemian soul, and a talented artist. The two were inseparable, especially when their sister had woes occupying her thoughts.

In the library, the brothers gathered, with Pearce pouring out generous measures of brandy to warm their bellies and calm their concerns.

"If there's one thing I am sure of," Lester confessed as he peered out of the large window, "it's that Finley is more than capable of looking after herself."

"Yes, you're right. We can trust one of Mimi's brothers to escort her back," said John, staring into space, swirling his glass of spirits.

Finley disappearing was not unusual. She was twenty-one years old and felt her whereabouts were often not worth troubling the household with.

Only Clive guessed correctly. He knew with certainty that Finley was not with Mimi. Rather, she was on her way to the Crimea.

"She has gone to find father."

Edward and John looked at him astounded.

"Lester forbade her," said John.

"She is not stupid enough to do that," snapped Edward.

"No, but she is brave enough," answered Clive.

*

Finley walked alongside the eclectic fleet of vessels moored against the wharf. Some were majestic sailing ships, others grubby, squat coal barges. A row of watermen's rowing boats was tethered to a rickety jetty in front of the pub. The hulls of the bigger ships groaned as their great wooden bulk accommodated the incessant movement of the water.

Under cover of darkness, she slipped past several men on the wharf. Some were in uniform guarding the ships and warehouses. Others seemed to linger, waiting for an opportunity to find a job or steal something that was inadvertently left behind.

"Who are you looking for, lad?" someone shouted gruffly.

At first, she didn't reply, not used to being addressed as a lad.

"Hey, laddie, I am talking to you."

Finley realised that he was calling her. She had a split second to think.

"I am sorry, Sir?" she called back, lowering her tone a little, hoping the sound would be suitably convincing.

"Who are you looking for? You seem lost. It's dangerous out here. Savage river pirates. Pilfering mudlarks and all that."

"I am looking for *The Mighty Bess.*"

"That's me. Who are you?"

"Fin Harrington."

"Sam told me to expect a woman."

"I am a woman," she said, returning to her normal vocal register, then pointing to the long locks disappearing into her bowler hat.

"Very well, then. Get on board. We sail at five o'clock. Best sit down there in the galley. Help yourself to some tea to warm you up."

Finley stared at the boat. She agreed with Sam Hudson's assessment. There was nothing mighty about 'Bess'. She was barely seaworthy. Her splintered wooden hull lacked a good coat of varnish. The metal funnel had seen better days. Ruckled rust patches had formed all over it. Captain Grainger noted the girl's scepticism.

"It has a furnace below. It's semi-steam and semi-sail. Bought it from old Keegan in Ireland. One of the first boats he built. Keegans are a good brand. Heard of 'em?"

"No, captain. Sorry."

"Not to worry, lass. Hop on board now, eh?"

Finley knew little about ships and boats, but she nodded in appreciation of the lesson.

"We will reach Calais before noon, Miss."

"Really?" questioned Finley, looking at the state of the ship.

Grainger looked crestfallen at her stunned expression.

"I mean, so quickly?"

"I have been doing this job for twenty-seven years. I can read the sea, sky, wind, and stars. It will be calm until we reach the mouth of the Thames, but as soon as we are in the channel, the wind will come up behind us and push us to

Calais. There will be some chop on the water, but the journey will be effortless. Steam and sail are a powerful combination."

The young crusader liked what she was hearing. The man was confident, which helped mitigate her misgivings about the ship. She decided Captain Grainger must have spent his life at sea. Rugged, with features hammered by the elements, his cap sat askew on his wild hair. A gnarly beard reached his chest. Above that, his pipe never left his mouth since he clenched it between his teeth when he spoke.

Finley was in her element, delighting in the new experience. The thought of going out to sea thrilled her. Better still, Grainger didn't blink an eye to her being a woman.

She poured herself a hot cuppa into a dented enamel mug. With a couple of extra sugars in it, it placated her growling stomach. She lay down on the wooden bench when she had finished, using her beloved Lester's scarf as a pillow. It smelled of his cologne. It reminded her of home. The thought jabbed her in the throat. She knew she had her reasons for leaving in the dead of night, but that didn't mean she wasn't concerned for her brothers' feelings.

As the bell of St Edward's chapel chimed out five deep dongs as the creaky old boat puttered and wove in between the ships that littered the Thames. It took some time to reach the mouth of the estuary.

The stowaway was awoken as the small vessel lurched into the choppier waters. Out in The Channel, the boat gained speed. Finley tottered her way up the stairs, sliding her hands up the rails, too scared to let go. Out on deck, Grainger was at the wheel, a horizontal plume of smoke puthering out of his mouth with each deep puff.

"Did the noise of the engine wake you? It's a busy waterway best crossed at a fast pace."

"This explains why we'll be there at noon," said Finley with a grin, her hair flapping across her face, getting caught in her smile.

At first, Finley was transfixed by the ship's bow, proudly cutting its way through the waves, then she remembered her manners.

"Tea, skipper?"

"Aye, go on then, lass."

As Captain Grainger had promised, she arrived in Calais just before noon. The wind had been at their back, filling the tattered sails. The thumping lump of an engine assisted nature, pushing them ahead toward the French mainland.

As Finley climbed onto the jetty, Grainger noted that the girl had a grace about her. The gnarly sea dog shook his head. He was far too old to admire young women.

8

PARIS

A drab concrete jetty ran out into The Channel, shielding the harbouring boats. Off in the distance, a prettier lighthouse stood alone, overlooking the scene. The small pier jutting out into the harbour was packed with people. Some were passengers waiting to depart. Others were waiting for loved ones.

It had rained that night, and the sand on the beach looked wet, tinting it brown. The small beach was littered with tiny holiday huts, so lovely for the summertime.

Finley wove her way through the hordes, trying her best not to mow their legs down with the corners of her case.

The town loomed ahead, its pale, prominent civic buildings contrasting with dark narrow streets and tumbled-down sailor's inns. There were factories in abundance. On a smaller scale, lace-makers sat in front of their humble houses, twisting and twining tens of bobbins until they had created the perfect patterns destined to adorn dresses all over the world. The homes beyond the town were typical of the French countryside, whitewashed with dark slate roofs. Where the houses stood on large plots, thick hedges or a row of poplars protected them.

With a rumbling stomach reminding her she had not eaten since arriving in London, she found a cafe and ordered a cheap meal of bread and tea.

Walking along the seafront, she stood looking out over The Channel while seagulls pestered her for crumbs. Hustlers constantly harassed her, eager to sell her accommodation in this or that inn. She wondered if the men luring her would have been as tenacious if they knew she was a woman. The longer she stayed hidden under the hat and coat, the more her confidence grew in her disguise.

Invigorated, it was the first time she had travelled this far by herself, and she was experiencing everything from a new perspective. Touring France with her father had been a more formal affair of coaches, trains, and hotels. It was liberating to be alone and anonymous, without any idea of what tomorrow would bring. Looking about, she saw a signpost for the station. 'At least the next step is clear.'

The French weren't a warm nation. They didn't harbour much fondness for the English. Finley found it ironic that the Francophiles had never forgiven the British for Waterloo, but the two countries were happy to ally themselves in the Crimean War.

The French had mastered the art of being difficult. The clerk at the train station complicated the transaction to such a degree that she considered taking a coach instead. Time was of the essence, and she needed to reach her father. She longed to chastise the little man, but he would become more spiteful and slower still, and that would mean missing the train.

With the ticket clamped between her lips, she yanked her case off the floor and ran down the concourse, looking for the right platform.

As she made her way alongside the carriages looking for a space, the platform guard screamed at her to hurry up and board. Her temper frayed a little further. *'Next time I will travel through Spain instead of France. That's if any of Europe still exists after this rotten war.'* As months turned to years, the battles raged on. Everyone prayed that no more countries would join the fight. Gloomy articles in the papers warned it could result in a war that could stretch from Russia to Spain and the countries of northern Africa.

The regular puffing of the engine increased in pace as the metal wheels squealed against the rails. Smoke wafted past the window, and the subtle smell of burning coal filled her nostrils.

Finley looked out at the French countryside. It was vast, flat, and distinctly ordinary. The train chuffed its way through tiny rural villages, with gleeful children looking over fences, waving wildly. Although the architecture differed, the tiny French houses reminded her of the small hamlets in England. Basic, functional, and often in need of repair, they were nothing like her home. It dawned on her that poverty was universal. Guilt stung her eyes. Sheer luck had meant that she had been born into a middle-class family, with far fewer hardships to endure. *'What if God randomly drops souls into bodies, then tosses them down to earth to get on with life, to sink or swim.'*

*

The centre of Paris came into focus as the train rumbled over a bridge. Looking down the Seine, the immense towers of Notre Dame, sitting squat on its own island, reached for the sky. The French capital was mesmerising, its bold architecture, the intricate sculptures that told ancient stories, and the mass of church steeples that soared towards the skyline.

She followed the path of the river until she reached the Gare de Lyon. The station was housed in a modern building that looked like a huge warehouse.

Pulling her case from the luggage rack, she negotiated the steps, then scouted the platform for signs to the ticket office.

The queue at the kiosk was long. Her arm ached, and soon her precious case was placed on the floor, only to be picked up when it was time to inch forward again. Nervously, she adjusted her coat collar and checked not a wisp of hair had worked itself loose. After a painful wait, finally, it was time to be served. She cleared her throat then spoke, planning to use as few words as possible.

"Bonjour."

The cantankerous Frenchman grunted in reply. By now, Finley was convinced that this rudeness was a national characteristic best ignored.

"Pardon, monsieur?"

His rapid yelled response did nothing to help her understand. *'Would he have been that rude if he knew I was a woman? I think not.'*

"Marseille, oui?"

The man tutted as he wrote out her destination on a simple white card. Grabbing the handle of an official-looking stamp, he rocked it on the squelchy ink pad. The stamp landed with a thud so forceful Finley could feel it make the windowsill shudder. The man flicked his wrist, and the ticket slid like a toboggan across the counter, so fast it skidded off the edge. Finley lurched at it as it fluttered towards the floor.

The ticket was useless for planning her departure, the details too vague. A kindly Dutch woman who had been behind her in the queue approached.

"Monsieur, your train will leave from platform
twelve at eight o'clock tonight."

A relieved Finley thanked her with a nod. After visiting the bureau de change, she decided to explore. Tiny colourful cafes, tobacconists, and news vendors had established themselves along with the main platform. Violins and harpsichords played haunting tunes in minor keys while chefs stood at the doorways of each little bistro and lured customers with the speciality of the day. The menus always included the French staples of onion soup, bread, and cheese. It intrigued her that while the British served everything with tea, the French served everything with wine.

Pointing her gloved hand at the menu, she chose some bread and cheese, thinking whatever was left over after the hunger pangs faded could easily be stored as a snack for later.

She dug her hand into her coat pocket and fished out a few coins.

Moments later, a smartly dressed waiter with a starched white shirt and glossy black waistcoat glided between the tables, arm aloft, holding a silver platter.

The items were swiftly transferred to her table, along with the customary glass of wine. Finley was in two minds about drinking it, then threw caution to the wind. Sipping at the deep red liquid, the colour of the darkest of rubies. It was warm and comforting. The golden bread was delicious, but the cheese took her breath away. Crumbly and pungent, it was nothing like the smooth, creamy wax she ate at home. Ravenous, nothing was kept for later.

After dining, Finley meandered to the relevant platform and collapsed onto a bench, gripping her case. A feeling of well-being engulfed her, and she dozed off, chin on chest. She didn't hear the train arrive and was awoken by someone shaking her.

"If you're going to Marseille, you had better wake up," said a man with a deep voice.

"Thank you," she mumbled as her head snapped back, but the man was already gone.

Grabbing her suitcase, she ran down the dimly-lit platform, fretting when she remembered she was supposed to meet Samuel's contact, Mr Craddick. Now, there was no time to find him. It was too late.

As Craddick was a unique name, she decided she should try and find the man on the train, failing that in Marseille. She fumed at her carelessness. *'Now, things will be much more difficult.'*

Reaching the door for her carriage, she scooted up the small iron steps. Her suitcase was swung into the rack above her head. She patted the plushly upholstered bench seat, which would also serve as her bunk, then made herself comfortable. Still exhausted from all the travel and a fitful night's sleep on Grainger's ship, her eyes fluttered closed again.

Suddenly, the carriage door swung open violently, and a leather suitcase came flying through the air. It landed on the floor in front of Finley, skidded down the thin aisle, then crashed against the far wall.

The suitcase was followed by a dishevelled man wearing a flannel tunic and a ragged woollen jersey. The neck of the jumper reached his chin. His scuffed leather boots reached his knees. A brown caped overcoat covered the whole sorry lot. To top it off, he had a brown fedora hat that had seen better days.

His hat and coat landed in the corner with one throw. Disrobing revealed a ruggedly handsome face with black eyes and wavy hair. He wore two days stubble, and it suited him.

Removing a fob watch, he looked at the time, then gave an almost silent whistle before muttering a curse-laded comment about his tardiness.

Finley watched him slump onto the bunk opposite her, then reach into his pocket. A battered notebook appeared and began to write in the dim light of an oil lamp hanging above him. Eventually, he lifted his head and looked at her.

"Français?"

"English," grunted Finley.

"Where are you going?"

He was abrupt, but the lilting Irish accent was lovely.

"Scutari."

The train left the station and charged into the black night. The moon rode high and lit up the countryside as they raced past the open fields, forests, hills, disturbing sleepy villages.

The man didn't say a word for the rest of the journey. Turning sideways as he sat, he squashed his coat and hat into a bundle as a makeshift pillow. Finley began to understand why his clothes looked the way they did. The curious fellow lay down on the seat and pulled his scarf over his head. Whether he had fallen into a slumber was unclear.

Finley was comfortable, pleased with the selection of items she had pilfered the family's cupboards. Her stepmother's light fur coat furled up under her head was warm and soft, and the overcoat made for a good blanket. As soon as she lay her head down, she fell asleep.

During the early hours of the morning, the Irishman had to answer the call of nature. He stood up and shuffled to the door. Finley didn't hear a thing. She lay peacefully, illuminated by the moonlight that streamed through the window. Her long hair had tumbled around her face as her bowler hat rocked gently on the floor. He looked down at her, so serene and so beautiful. He put her in her she was in her early twenties.

'Is she really off to that hellhole Scutari? She doesn't have the look of a nurse about her. And nurses do not wear suits. They wear uniforms. Maybe it's an excuse to escape a domineering

or a cruel husband? Trust Samuel to complicate my life. This is one distraction that I don't need.'

*

On reaching Marseille, he was the first to disembark. He threw his battered luggage out onto the platform, narrowly missing the station manager. The outraged official threatened him with the Gendarmerie. The Irishman gave a slight bow and a pretend apologetic smile.

Finley climbed off the train lithely, hat pulled down, collar pulled up. *'I wonder what she looks like in a dress.'*

"Follow me," he told her gruffly.

"No, thank you. I can see my way to a hotel."

"If you intend to get to Scutari, I suggest you follow me."

"If you insist." said the girl, hoping to give the man the slip outside the station.

"By the way, I'm Finley Harrington."

"I know," said Craddick.

9

THE PHOTOGRAPH

Eleanor Harrington was delighted that Lord and Lady Paxton had invited her to their country home north of London. It was a pleasant surprise to be in the presence of so many cultured people. The house had four wings, and there were enough rooms to accommodate over fifty visitors for the weekend. Most of the stately crowd were aristocrats or government ministers. Tories abounded. No prominent industrialists were in attendance. The nouveau riche were considered common. The weekend was about tradition and class, not upstarts and entrepreneurs. Lady and Lord Paxton understood who were fitting guests and who were not.

She waltzed into the marble-tiled entrance hall, her eyes drawn to the grand mahogany staircase. The landing floor was lined with thick exotic carpets. A twinge of envy coursed through her veins.

When she had married a commissioned officer, she believed that he was a man of status, and he would follow the conventions of upper-class society. She was sorely disappointed when she realised that her Colonel husband was more scholarly than social, and worse, a self-made man in the army. There was no string of aristocratic generals in his bloodline, stretching back to Blenheim and beyond. An infantry sergeant for a father was about as low as things could get.

Lady Paxton had decorated her vast country house for Christmas. Every room displayed a majestic tree. The beautiful pines stretched from floor to ceiling and filled the house with the most delightful aroma. The trees were dotted with a breath-taking display of tasteful decorations.

"I got the baubles in Venice, Eleanor," Lady Paxton.

"I see. How lovely," Eleanor said, hoping not to be asked about an Italian tourist trap she had yet to visit.

"The world-famous glass blowers guided me to choose an assortment of jewel-coloured delights. I specified the shapes and sizes, then they made them to order and got a man to bring them. Fabulous, aren't they?"

Eleanor nodded and smiled. Her jaw, locked with jealousy, couldn't be moved to speak.

There were baubles of every shape and size, including the most delicate multicoloured glass angels.

"Between you and me," the lady whispered, "an important person at Buckingham Palace loves them. So much so she almost accepted them as a gift."

Lady Paxton's raised eyebrows and Cheshire cat grin confirmed that 'the person' had to be the queen herself.

Tiny candles flickered on the tree. The baubles reflected tinted light, which bounced off every shiny surface in the room. The result was an enchanting ambience. Eleanor felt her chest restrict, and a sensation grip her larynx. Oh, how she coveted the woman's home and lifestyle. Even with the lump of resentment sitting in her throat, Eleanor had the grace to complement Lady Paxton on her exceptional taste and creativity.

The warm atmosphere of yuletide bliss enveloped the house party. Elegant women floated from room to room in silk gowns and fur stoles, eager to savour every luxury that their generous hostess offered, desperate to relay their experiences to those friends who were excluded from the event.

"We only have space for a limited number of guests," whispered Lady Paxton behind her hand. "I repeatedly tell Lord Paxton that the suites are insufficient. I do hope he builds another wing soon."

Eleanor smiled and agreed, but her mouth quivered at the edges, and she hoped that Lady Paxton didn't see it.

"The limited space does add a particular exclusivity to the weekend, my dear," she told Eleanor. "We have to disappoint so many of our friends. We must be quite particular of whom we associate with."

Eleanor excused herself to recharge her glass. From the giant bay windows, she saw the light dusting of snow outside, bolstering the festive atmosphere within. The satisfaction with her lot in life was falling as swiftly as the soft snowflakes.

Lady Paxton had catered for every eventuality. The men went out to shoot grouse at daybreak while the ladies casually sat about making small talk and gossiping. On the men's return just before luncheon, the group reconvened for wholesome and warming eggnog, mince pies and sherry. During the afternoon, they played bridge and backgammon. Some gambling took place in Lord Paxton's study, but nobody spoke of it. It was men's business, and they kept it hush-hush.

Always a great social occasion, this year Lady Paxton had invited a photographer to record the festivities. She discussed the booking gleefully with her husband over breakfast.

"I shall be the first hostess to ever publish a Daguerreotype in the social column of the newspaper."

"As you wish, my dear."

"It will add even more prestige to the event."

Lord Paxton smiled politely, then focused on buttering his toast. He was far more reticent than his wife, preferring a quiet life. She loved the idea of having her name and face in the newspaper. For her, column-inches were the perfect way to show off and snub her enemies at the same time.

General Logan stared at Eleanor from across the broad dining table. If the top had been any bigger, he would have needed a telescope. Her grace and beauty captivated him. His late wife had been such a contrast. In his opinion, she had been a   dowdy, miserable matron. For him was a reason, rather than an excuse, to support the most elite and extravagant brothels around the world. Even so, it had been a long time since he had been with a woman, and the idea that a beauty like Eleanor would consider his company was a compliment. Yes, she was married to Harrington, but they would be discreet. Secretly, the general pondered what he might do to rid her of her husband.

After their encounter at the Harrington family home, Logan was convinced that Eleanor had subtly suggested that she would be delighted to spend time with him. It was unusual for a married woman to attend a weekend in the country without her husband, but Lady Paxton had insisted on her attendance.

"My husband and I will chaperone you," she encouraged Eleanor Harrington. "You will be in safe hands."

*

General Logan and Eleanor Harrington had been making modest small talk all evening. Very few people had noticed their fleeting flirtations. When there was a lull in the festive atmosphere, Lady Paxton chose that moment to gather everybody together.

"I have some exciting news! Something very special is happening in thirty minutes. Something quite spectacular. Ladies, you have half an hour to powder yourselves. I know you will want to look magnificent. Gentlemen, please join my husband for brandy and cigars."

The puzzled crowd dispersed. Lady Paxton gave a confirming nod to her accomplice as the guests trooped back to the hall as the clock struck the hour. He lugged a curious wooden box in front of the group.

"Come now, everyone. Gather together on the staircase, please," barked William Bambridge, the photographer.

*

The flash exploded like a bomb, leaving the stunned crowd blinking.

"And?" a shrill voice asked in the man's ear.

"It will be perfect, Lady Paxton. People will remember this photo for years."

William packed the glass frames into a special box.

"Please excuse me, everyone. I must take these to my studio and develop them as soon as possible."

Lady Paxton grabbed the man discreetly by the arm.

"And you will hand them straight over to The Times forthwith? Just as we discussed?"

"Yes, ma'am."

Little did they know that the photograph William Bambridge had just taken would create a phenomenal furore.

True to his word, Bembridge dropped the image off just as the newspaper office opened in the morning. He barely had time to inspect his work, merely to develop it.

The editor, John Thadeus Delane, was far more alert than the photographer. Beyond composition and depth of field, he saw the true meaning. He spied the offence immediately.

He took to his typewriter and penned a piece to accompany the photograph. He yanked the paper out from the roller and sprinted to the typesetters' office.

"Urgent this piece. Needs to be in the morning's edition, Gerald. With this image."

"Right you are, boss."

Knowing that he would sell more newspapers on the next day than he had all year, Delane doubled the print run, then sat back and waited.

*

Eleanor Harrington had been appointed a room in the south wing. Light and warm, most of the elite guests had been allocated rooms there. She felt privileged. As she made her way upstairs, Eleanor Harrington heard footsteps behind her on the landing. She turned to see who it was.

"I apologise, Eleanor. I didn't mean to give you a fright," said General Logan, his voice dripping charm.

She looked at the smartly turned-out military man and gave him a dazzling smile.

"Not at all, Sir. It's always a pleasure to see you. I hoped that we would meet again," she purred.

"Oh, my dear, you read me so well."

"You made your intentions amply clear on the staircase," she answered in a low sensual voice, hoping she sounded available to him.

General Logan had become an extraordinarily rich man by winning wars. All that the queen demanded was victory. When he succeeded in giving her the head of the enemy on a plate, she rewarded him handsomely. The general had no children, and his vast estate lay untouched.

The scheming woman had things all worked out. If Eleanor could seduce and marry him after Ernest died in Crimea, her new spouse could provide her with a small fortune. There would be complications getting remarried, but she didn't have to marry him in England. They could do that in the Orient.

The staff of the great house had turned down the lamps, leaving just enough light for guests to navigate the long corridors. Eleanor looked beautiful in the soft glow of the bedside oil lamp. Her hair was curled into perfect ringlets, her flawless white décolletage was luscious and inviting, and her thickly powdered face and large baby blue eyes were veiled with long, seductive lashes.

After ensuring that nobody was watching, General Logan sneaked back towards Eleanor's bedroom and gave three subtle taps with his knuckle. Inside, the fire was glowing, and it perpetuated the romantic mood. In his early sixties, he was thick about the middle, but his legs and arms were skinny. The soldier's physique of his youth had faded. In the shadows of the room, as he removed his clothes, he looked like a fat stick man. Eleanor was a middle-aged woman who had never borne children. Her body was taught and flawless. The general almost moaned with the delicious sight of her. *'Ernest Harrington is— or was—a lucky man.'*

Anthony Logan clambered onto the bed and began kissing her. His dreadful moustache smelled of cigar smoke and tasted of brandy. As much as she disliked Ernest, he was at least a handsome man and an excellent lover, although that had ended years ago. It was a major setback that Ernest had five children. Not short of heirs, he lost physical interest in his wife as she lost financial interest in him. Things could have been different, but they weren't.

Eleanor switched off the part of her brain that handled her senses and ramped up the part that plotted and schemed.

'When I settled into a more permanent relationship with the general, his passion and interest will. That allows me to pursue somebody younger and more attractive in my spare time.'

The general had become flaccid with age, but eventually, after much grunting, groaning, and coaxing, his body stiffened. He lumbered over her then collapsed his whole weight on her. For Eleanor, it was not important to be satisfied, and she patronised him by insisting that he was the most indulgent lover that she had ever enjoyed. This was her greatest betrayal of her husband.

*

Lady Paxton ordered her butler to be in the village when the train that delivered the newspapers arrived. The poor chap had stood in the cold from the early hours of the morning in fear that he would miss the delivery. Looking out of the dining-room window onto the long driveway, she saw him slowly trudging back through the snow. For once, she bent the rules, and she banged on the glass and beckoned him to hurry up.

"Here you are, ma'am."

The lady of the house almost rugby tackled him to the floor to grab hold of the early morning edition, so keen was she to read.

"That will be all, thank you," she said dismissively.

She threw the broadsheet across the table and began to read. With trepidation, Lord Paxton looked over her shoulder.

The weekend was declared a grand success. The social column extolled Lady Paxton for outdoing herself for the fifth year in a row, which had been voted the most prestigious of the festive season for each of those years.

Self-satisfied, Lady Paxton continued to read, delighted to have so many public accolades. All of a sudden, her eyes widened, and her cheeks turned bright red. Her airs and graced vanished as she swore like a common navvy. A savage guttural shriek followed before she began to sob uncontrollably and fled from the room.

Lord Paxton searched for the offensive lines. In the last paragraph of the article, the columnist noted General Logan and Eleanor Harrington's inappropriate behaviour. Nobody could challenge the evidence. The photograph didn't lie. General Logan had been ill-prepared. The flash had exploded unexpectedly. Shocked and wide-eyed, he was caught in the act of fondling Mrs Eleanor Harrington's right breast. The article didn't have to go any further than "inappropriate." The image was more than self-explanatory.

It was the social faux pas of the decade. From the moment that edition of The Times appeared on the street, tongues began to wag. Lady Paxton was mortified. She fantasised about buying every copy and burning it. Under her stamping feet, the glass plates would be crushed to a thin powder, like wheat ground between millstones. She would pay anything for the photograph to be destroyed.

On the pavement outside the paper's headquarters, a hopeful public lined up to see the real daguerreotype. The editor could pluck a suitably high price out of the air, and he would still sell out.

"This is madness, boss," said Gerald, as he counted the number of heads in the snaking queue on the pavement below.

"And lucrative, Gerald. This is going to be the most profitable year the newspaper has ever had."

The traditional welcoming of the advent of the Christmas season was turned into a circus. Lady Paxton's name was associated with adultery and debauchery, and for those that she had snubbed in the past, there were mutterings of the word 'orgy'. For all the mock disgust, the upper class loved the salaciousness of it all. It was pure gutter-press entertainment, more akin to a piece found in a penny dreadful than a respectable broadsheet with a prestigious pedigree.

The commoners had a field day. The poor relished any story that displayed the aristocracies' true colours. Lady Paxton, General Logan and Mrs Eleanor Harrington were the laughing stock of the squalid tenements. Tearing the image out from the paper, it was put up on display in every pub, tavern, and inn across the realm. The poor, homeless, starving, illiterates of every slum in England had a jolly good belly laugh at the toffs' expense. The photograph didn't lie.

*

Eleanor Harrington opened The Times at the same moment as Lady Paxton. Within an instant, the gold-digger went from famous to infamous. All her plans for a cosy life with General Logan were shattered. Her future flashed before her eyes. If, and when he found out, Ernest would evict her—in the meantime, his sons would hound her out.

To save her reputation, she pondered escaping to a colony. Alas, she knew that word travelled fast, and she wouldn't outrun the scandal for long. Knowing it was pointless to try and hide the matter, she flung the morning newspaper down in horror and fled to the safety of her bedroom. Lying on her bed, face buried into the luxury duck down pillows, she cried hysterically.

*

"What was that all about?" asked Lester, back from Southampton after hearing about Finley's disappearance.

"She was reading the newspaper, then rushed off in tears," answered Clive. "Perhaps she read of a friend's death in the obituary column."

Edward picked up the paper and began paging through it. Something had to explain Eleanor's frantic exit. He didn't have to thumb through far. The revealing article was on the inside page.

"Good Heavens! This is the first time I can say
that I agree with our stepmother. This is worth
crying over. I hope she has a jolly good howl
before I physically throw her out of the house."

Clearing his throat, he began to read the feature aloud. The
other brothers' jaws dropped further the longer Edward
continued.

"What a bloody embarrassment," said Lester.
"After that visit, we know that Eleanor wishes
father dead. It's of no surprise that she is
courting Logan. She is hoping to marry him if
father—."

"I can't believe she has lined up her next
conquest," said Edward, banging his fist on the
table.

"The bloody shrew!" cursed Clive, a man who
rarely used foul language. "She has to leave here
immediately. What say you chaps? How can she
stay? Being a loose woman whilst father risks his
life for the nation!"

Lester tried to be the voice of reason.

"As if we don't have enough to worry about with
Finley's disappearance, now we have this
distraction. We have every police officer in the
country looking for her, while our selfish
stepmother disgraces us, gallivanting in public
with another man—"

A solemn John interrupted.

"I am terrified that Finley has been murdered. I can't sleep at night thinking she's lying dead in a ditch somewhere. We have scoured every piece of open land in and around the house and found nothing. I arranged for her scent to be given to a pack of hounds. Still nothing."

"I have told you repeatedly, Finley is on her way to Crimea to find papa. You are looking for her in the wrong place," snapped Clive. "Stop worrying about Finley and get this harlot out of our home!"

The words were hardly out of his mouth when the library door opened, and Mr Pearce appeared, letter in hand.

"This letter is addressed to you, Lester. I don't want to get your hopes up, but judging by the postmark, perhaps it is from the French Army. There might be some good news from the Russian Front?"

Lester jumped up and took the letter. *'Hmm. Paris.'* He doubted that the French Army would ever send him a letter, but some news was better than no news. With misplaced optimism, he ripped the envelope open, hopeful that Mr Pearce's guess was correct. The letter was short and to the point.

Dear Brothers

I couldn't wait for the army to rescue father.

The idea of him suffering as a prisoner is hideous.

I am safe, and I will post a letter from the next city that I reach.

Your loving sister,

Fin

Lester flung the letter across the table at Clive.

"How did you know? Did she tell you? Have you kept this a secret from us? I have a good mind to throttle you here and now."

"How dare you! Clearly, you don't know your sister the way that I do."

"Stop it, both of you," ordered John," Clive's gut instinct was correct, and we were too stubborn to listen to him."

"We are a bunch of cowards. Our sister is doing our job for us, and she did it without flinching. We should be ashamed of ourselves."

The others looked at Clive in embarrassment. His words rang true. They knew that their father lost, missing, or wounded, yet, they had discounted acting because it would endanger their own lives.

"I'm sorry, Clive," consoled Lester, putting a hand on his brother's shoulder.

"You were all happy to wait for an indifferent government to take their time in finding papa—even when General Logan had warned them that the British Army wouldn't search the area until the spring."

A gloomy atmosphere developed, and nobody spoke. Each one was quiet, lost in his own thoughts. They loved their sister dearly. They had done everything together from an early age, but now, they were a fractious, fractured family.

"Do you think she'll make it to Crimea?" John asked.

"Of course, she will," answered Clive," I have no doubt in my mind."

"But how?"

"You know what she's like when she gets an idea in her head. She can be so determined."

"You mean reckless and foolhardy," added Lester.

"Stop it," Clive warned.

"We will contact the authorities. Mount a search in France and monitor passenger manifests."

Clive shook his head at Lester. His brothers had learnt nothing.

'You won't find her because she doesn't want to be found.'

*

It was a morning of intense drama in the Harrington household. The brothers thought that they had seen the last of Eleanor for the day, but she came into the library to find them, looking anxious and harassed. Her embarrassment was obvious, and Lester was surprised that she was brave enough to show her face. Edward, ever the gentleman, stood up as she walked in. John ignored her completely. Clive was in a dark mood. Just the sight of the woman vexed him, let alone speaking to her.

"I—I would never betray your father," Eleanor stammered.

The four men said nothing, and she continued.

"You must believe me. It is all a dreadful mistake. I was unaware that his hand was on my—"

She didn't finish the sentence. The brothers felt embarrassed. They didn't want to hear the intimate details of their stepmother's experience.

"The general is an honourable, decorated war hero. He would never take advantage of me. Besides, I would never allow it."

Nobody could respond. They didn't know what to say to her. Eleanor was desperate to be exonerated, but no one was willing to give her the benefit of the doubt. Afraid, guilty, and humiliated, she began to lash out.

"Say something," she shrieked. "At least tell me that you believe me! I demand a reply. Why are you punishing me for something that isn't my fault?"

The woman paced around the room like an angry caged bear in a zoo.

"I suppose you will tell your father about it?

Nothing. She jabbed an accusing finger at the quartet.

"Which one of you will go out of your way to brand me an adulterer?"

Their silence pushed Eleanor's tongue dangerously out of control. That was the moment the point of no return was breached.

"You don't know what it is like to be married to a perfect man. You don't know what it is to live in a house where my husband loves his children more than me," she screamed. "I am entitled to some happiness, and General Logan treats me well."

They looked at her aghast. Eleanor clapped both hands over her mouth, realising she had just incriminated herself.

"You will leave this house tonight. We don't care where you go or what you do. You will leave a letter for our father, allowing him to take legitimate steps to rid himself of you. Take whatever belongs to you and get out. We don't want a trace of anything that reminds us of you. We will continue without you like you never existed."

Lester had finally got to say what he longed to for so many years. He put his hands in his pockets, dropped his head, and left the room. His brothers watched him leave. It was the perfect summation. They didn't need to add to it.

The truth had set Eleanor free. She was free to live anywhere except in the house of Colonel Ernest Harrington.

10

MARSEILLE

Marseille was a different world. Finley found it hard to believe that she was still in France. Her eyes soaked up every detail of her glamorous surroundings. When something entertained her, she felt the heavy burden of conscience as she reminded herself that she was not on holiday but on a journey to find her father. If it had been otherwise, she would have booked into a hotel that overlooked the port, sat on the balcony, and studied the diverse cultures that bustled around the ancient city.

Marseille housed the French Navy. The city was teeming with dandy little officers in clean uniforms, marching about like little Napoleons. The Naval officers enjoyed being admired. She found them entertaining and wondered if they performed as well in battle.

The streets close to the harbour were awash with people from all over the world. Orientals teemed at the docks, their ships delivering tea, spice, and opium. North Africans in their ankle-length shirts loaded cargo while Arab ship owners sat at tables smoking shisha pipes and drinking mint tea. They looked relaxed, but it was a ploy. They watched their ships with the same intensity as falcons, the birds that they revered.

The British had abolished slavery in 1833 and had paid compensation to their masters. For once, the government could hold their heads aloft. They had bought the freedom of a lot of people. But the abhorrent practice had not been abolished everywhere, and Finley's blood ran cold wondering if the large Arab ships contained a human cargo. She recalled that France had abolished slavery earlier than the British. It was doubtful that slave traders would be as brazen as to dock in a French port.

The dark-skinned Moors, exiled from Spain, were dark, dignified people. Indians traded with Jews, both peoples of ancient nations, well versed in the art of bargaining. The Indian women wore vibrant silk saris and chirruped like birds among themselves. The Sardinians were intriguing. Their women displayed unusual headdresses and embroidered clothing, while the men, with their long caps, had inherited the Italian flair for finery.

Finley was unprepared for the scourge of pickpockets and petty thieves. The gipsy women were treacherous, selling brass rings as gold to anybody naïve enough to believe them. Pickpockets were as rampant as rats. As much as people loathed them, they had to admire their skill. They could steal your coat, shoelaces, and money within a few seconds. They were more talented at sleight-of-hand than magicians.

Finley followed Gabriel Craddick at a distance. She watched as he confidently heaved his way through the congested harbour, head and shoulders above the throng. Finally, he stopped at a small Arabic coffee house and sat down at a table on the pavement. When she reached him, she pulled out her own chair.

"Watch your suitcase," was all he said to her.

Gabriel ordered coffee and an aromatic spicy dish that Finley couldn't identify.

"Eat. It's going to be a long day," he told her.

"Are you in the habit of giving orders, or are you just very rude?" Finley asked.

"Are you one of those spoiled brats who struggle to do as they are told because they have had a bevy of servants catering to their whims?"

"Will you treat me any better if I apologise for my pedigree?"

She stared at him, waiting for an answer, but there was none. They ignored each other, but Gabriel was impressed that she was brave enough to fight back and had not wilted into tears.

Her reply was powerful. It was clear she could look after herself. He was relieved that she was not what he called 'a chirper', one of those women who couldn't stop talking. Finley ordered coffee and the same dish as Gabriel. Her food arrived, and she began to eat without delay. Finley didn't criticise the spoon she was given, the lack of table-cloth or the carafe of cheap wine. She was ravenous. He expected her eyes to begin watering and complain that her mouth was on fire, but she didn't. She wolfed it down with great relish.

"That was delicious. What was it?" she asked.

"It's a Moroccan dish, cooked in a tajine. Dates, vegetables, sour milk, and goat,"

Gabriel expected her to heave, but she didn't.

"I enjoyed the spices. Restaurants should make this at home. It's a lot better than bland meat and watery vegetables."

She drank her coffee and lounged on the rickety chair without saying a word. Behind her, Finley could hear two men having a heated debate in French. Picking up bits and pieces of what they said, she decided it was about money and debt. As the conversation became louder and angrier, the face-to-face shouting began. Arms waved. Spittle flew.

Nobody at the coffee shop paid any attention to them. These kinds of arguments were regular occurrences between the overly emotional French who had no stiff upper lip. Within seconds, the two men were on their feet. One man grabbed the other by his collar. They were cursing loudly, something about their mothers, which was more shocking than the brutal physical violence they inflicted on each other.

A scuffle ensued. By now, the men on the pavement had had their fill of the hooligans and were stepping in to separate them. Everyone was shouting at once. Finley heard a whistle. The gendarmerie had been alerted, and she could see two policemen running through the dense crowd, but they were still far away.

The two men got closer and closer to Finley. When they were virtually on top of her, they lost their footing and rammed into her. It was so hard that Finley's fragile chair rocked from side to side, its old wooden legs creaking and bending under the strain. The chair splintered into a hundred pieces, and Finley crashed to the floor. Gabriel jumped to his feet and rushed forward. He grabbed one hooligan and hit him in the stomach. It was a powerful blow, and the man doubled over. The gendarmes were getting close, the whistle piercing the air in a high trembling note. In the furore, nobody noticed a third man at Gabriel's table. He bent down and took the Irishman's suitcase. The thief began to run. The brawlers scattered, separated, and disappeared as fast as they had arrived.

The entire event took no more than three minutes. Gabriel had fallen for the oldest trick in the book. While he had been distracted, they had stolen his suitcase.

Gabriel roared, furious with himself for being so stupid and not recognising their well-rehearsed ploy. Then, he shouted some colourful Gaelic expletives.

Finley was already on her feet. She jumped on a chair closest to her and looked down the street. The thief was making one mistake. He was running. If he had been calm, the throng would have camouflaged him. She watched his head bobbing up and down as he wove through the crowd.

In a deft movement, Finley jumped off the chair, picked up her case, and gave chase. As she followed the robber, she was ahead of Gabriel by seventy-five yards. She chased the thief into a narrow lane and watched him turn up a dark alley.

Finley was running through a maze of cobbled streets and medieval buildings, clueless as to where she was. The thief heard her footsteps. He'd never been caught before, and he was determined that no one would imprison him. Up above, the ancient, buckled buildings loomed over her. Only a thin sliver of blue sky could light the narrow passageway.

She was about to surrender when she saw the suitcase standing in the middle of the alley. Thrilled that the pickpocket had given up, Finley walked to Gabriel's suitcase boldly and bent over to pick it up. Behind her, she heard the footsteps of her travelling companion. She didn't turn around or look up. Her eyes were on her prize. For the second time that day, the thief caught her off guard. All she heard was a tremendous crack, and the world went dark.

Finley's face hit the ground, her cheekbone smashing into the cobbles. Her hat rolled away, her scarf unravelled, and her hair framed her face like a halo. The pickpocket looked back once to see if his victim was fit to give chase. He stopped in his tracks. The young man was a woman, and she had the most beautiful face and the most striking long golden hair that he had ever seen.

Gabriel turned up the alley and saw Finley lying in a heap. He sprinted toward her, terrified that she was dead. After lifting her into his arms, he and began looking around, unsure which direction to follow. *'Perhaps I should take her back to the safer side of the city? Find a doctor who could assess the damage and bandage her up?'*

He was concerned that the thief would return—for the other man's sake more than his own. Yet, although he wanted to throttle the life out of the rogue, his first priority was the girl in his arms. Her wounds were severe. *'If I get her to a convent, perhaps the nuns would tend to her for a few days.'*

*

When Finley came around, a dull pulsating throb filled the inside of her head. Her scalp was bleeding, and the cut was raw. When she moved, the sharp pain made her panic, thinking her skull was cracked. Her hair, caked in blood, felt stiff and crispy against her skin. While she was conscious that someone was carrying her, she couldn't bear to lift her head to find out who. Feeling faint, everything was hazy and spun around her. Finally, Finley surrendered to unconsciousness. She couldn't struggle, even if her life depended on it.

*

Behind a small window, a hand let go of a curtain. A battered old door opened. The noise startled a vigilant and vulnerable Gabriel, staggering along with Finley on the wrong side of town. A person appeared, whom he could only describe as a small black ghost.

"Come," she said in French and grabbed his elbow.

The woman steered the Irishman into the kitchen, guiding him down three stone steps to an exceptionally clean kitchen, then pointed to a small bed in the corner. The ceiling was low, and he had to take care not to bump his head on the beams. As he lay Finley down on the soft eiderdown, Gabriel heard the ebony spectre run out of the tiny house. A few moments later, she returned with the suitcases.

"Thank you."

Finley's eyes fluttered weakly. All she could see was the ceiling above her. It had wide wooden beams. Above that were some badly fitted floorboards, and through the gaps, she could see into the room above. Eyes now half-open, she moved her head slightly and saw Gabriel standing over her.

Although blurriness impeded her vision, it was clear his expression was grim.

"Where am I?" Finley muttered.

The shadowy figure stepped forward and answered in a thick Arabian accent.

"My name is Fatima. You are in my home. Welcome."

Finley could barely nod her thankful response.

*

The patient must have fallen asleep because she was wakened by voices in the room. It took some time before Finley could register what they were discussing.

"We need to get to the harbour," said Finley weakly.

"It's too late. We have, er, missed the boat," answered Gabriel

"Oh no!"

She grunted and winced as she tried to push herself up onto her elbows.

"Lie down!" said Gabriel. "It is not the end of the world. We will find another boat."

"It is a matter of life and death," murmured Finley.

Gabriel shook his head.

"You are not going to die in Marseille and complicate my life," he told her gruffly.

"Where do you need to be?" asked Fatima.

"I am going to the Crimea to find my father. The British Army has forsaken him. He may be at a field hospital if he's lucky. There is a chance he is behind Russian enemy lines. Someone somewhere must be able to help. Whatever his fate, I will not leave him there to die alone."

Gabriel couldn't believe what he was hearing.

'So, this young woman has embarked on a journey to find her father behind enemy lines! Is she a lunatic? The area is huge! If the Russian soldiers capture her, they will give no thought to violating a lone British woman. She would never reach her father alive or sane.'

"Do you know what the risks are?" he snapped.

Finley closed her eyes and gave a solemn nod.

"Have you ever been with a man?"

Finley glared at his insolence. Fatima pretended not to hear such a shocking question.

"If you haven't, you will lay with at least thirty after the Russian soldiers are finished with you."

Disgusted in Gabriel, Fatima went to fill a basin with hot water.

"Leave us," she said. "I will wash her alone. Allez. Outside."

As soon as he closed the door, Fatima prepared to remove her burka.

"He is telling the truth. If the enemy don't kill or cripple you, afterwards, you will either be with child or never be able to conceive. I have seen it in my country."

As she uncovered her face, a beautiful woman appeared. Her thick dark hair hung down her back. She had soft brown, almond-shaped eyes framed with ebony lashes that contrasted gorgeously with her olive skin.

"Who is that man, Finley?"

"I have hired him to help me find a passage to the Black Sea."

"He is a caring man," said Fatima.

Finley couldn't reply. She was in too much pain as her wounds were tended to. Besides, she didn't think of Gabriel as caring, more of a cold, self-interested mercenary.

Fatima dabbed at the head wound with some vinegar. The slice in her scalp stung like a stroke from a headmaster's cane. She tried to grab at Fatima's hand but failed.

"Shush now. Keep still and let me look after you."

With the blood sponged out of her hair, Finley was given a clean shirt to wear. Her laboured movements and wincing expression were worrying.

"I will give you a tincture. It will take away the pain," Fatima told her. "Keep it with you, and don't take more than I tell you to. It is very bitter,

but you must keep it in your mouth for as long as
you can. If you take more, you will go to sleep
and never wake up again."

This idea didn't console Finley, but she swallowed the two
drops that she was allowed to. Fatima covered herself in
her burka once more and fetched Gabriel.

"What is your name, Sir?"

"Gabriel Craddick."

"Mmm," she nodded. "Yes, the messenger angel.
What have you come to tell me, Gabriel?"

She smiled at him with expectation, but Gabriel shook his
head.

"I know your Christian bible. Gabriel brought
word of the Christ child. It is almost your
Christmas."

"Er, yes. I suppose so. Now, can you tell me how
to reach the harbour from here?"

"It is better that I take you to the harbour, or you
will get lost or stabbed."

"Why will you be safe?"

"Our men are happy to cut the throat of a man
who hurts their wife and children. Everybody
knows that, and they leave us women alone."

"But the men will go to the guillotine for
murder," said Gabriel.

"They are prepared to die for their families."

Gabriel didn't ask any more questions. Fatima's answer left him ashamed. It took him to another time and place where he failed to protect the person he loved.

"Now, I will take you to my uncle. He will help you."

"I will carry Finley."

"No, I have a cart. We will put her on it and pull it."

She went to a humble cupboard and took out a black burka and hajib.

"We will cover you with this," she told Finley, enveloping her from head to toe in the garments.

Fatima thrust something else into Finley's hands, a finely embroidered silk kaftan.

"To sleep in. I will put it in your case."

"Now, we leave," Fatima told her two house guests.

Fatima smiled down at Finley

"Now nobody can see your face. Nobody knows who you are. It is a good feeling, yes?"

Finley gave a small nod. It was an incredibly good feeling being anonymous.

"I will take you to the old harbour," Fatima told Gabriel.

"Why?" Gabriel said with a frown. "All the ships there are local fishing vessels."

"My uncle, Assad Al Aziz, has a dhow in the harbour. It is a humble vessel but fit for the gruelling journey ahead. He will help you."

"How do we repay you and your family?" asked Gabriel.

"In our culture, we are taught to help the stranger. You owe us nothing. If I take your money, I dishonour Allah's commandment."

"Thank you," Gabriel said with sincerity.

Finley sat slumped over on the cart, her heart was thumping, and her head was spinning, hoping she would have the strength to grip on.

"We will pull the cart together, Gabriel. I will help you." Fatima told him.

"No. I will pull the cart by myself. In my culture, it is very rude to let women do arduous work if there is a man available to do it."

He gave her his special smile.

"I like your culture, " Fatima chuckled.

"You keep her covered," Fatima ordered Gabriel. "This is a beautiful woman with blonde hair. An Arab man will steal her for his harem."

Gabriel shook his head, *'What a bloody disaster this is. Thieves, sheikhs, harems, and a beautiful woman who was complicating his life. A short voyage had become bedlam.'*

*

Lester opened the telegram, read it, and passed it to his brothers.

REACHED MARSEILLE STOP SAFE STOP HAVE
AN EXPERIENCED GUIDE STOP FINLEY

"We need to follow her. I doubt she does have a guide. She's alone. There is bound to be trouble."

"Heaven knows who this guide is. It could be any old scoundrel," muttered Edward.

"Fin has a good nose for who a good chap is and who is a rascal," said Clive. "She grew up with us."

"Nevertheless, if she's not in danger now, she damned well will be when she gets to the Black Sea."

"You're right, Lester," John agreed. "Start packing, brothers. We need to take the next steamer to Calais."

"Do you think that Fin took the paddle steamer from Dover?"

"I doubt it," Clive replied. "It would have been far too slow!"

"Perhaps we should find another way to get there," said Lester.

"I doubt we can. We aren't as creative as our sister," chuckled Clive.

"What if this male guide takes advantage of her?" Edward asked quietly, embarrassed.

Nobody replied. The risks were clear, no matter how headstrong and invincible their self-sufficient little sister thought she was.

The gloomy ambience ended when Mr Pearce came into the library and politely approached Lester.

"It is officially the Christmas season. Would you like us to begin decorating the house accordingly?"

"No, thank you, Mr Pearce. The staff may celebrate Christmas as they wish below stairs. This year, our family will not be celebrating Christmas in the usual way."

11

A DHOW TO MALTA

A Turkish guard paced the dhow's deck, carrying a cutlass at his hip. It was fastened with an ostentatious leather belt, studded with gold and silver medallions. Its ornate hilt was beaten silver and embedded with precious stones designed to resemble a falcon. The curved silver blade was polished until it gleamed like a mirror and honed until it was razor-sharp. It was designed to be as much of a warning as a weapon: stay away because this guard works for a very wealthy and powerful man.

The moment Fatima put her foot onto the gangplank, the guard intercepted her. He was abrupt and talked to her aggressively. The language that the guard spoke was deep, guttural Arabic. The guard's voice became louder and more demanding until he decided that she was not a threat.

Once calm, he listened to her.

"I am here to see my uncle, Assad Al Aziz."

The guard was perplexed. It was the man's first night aboard the dhow, and he was having great difficulty identifying all the members of the Al Aziz family. He disappeared for a short while and came back with two women and gave them instructions to identify Fatima as their cousin. Amal and Maryam wore hajibs, but their faces were uncovered.

"Who are these people?" asked Maryam in Arabic.

"Mr Craddick and Miss Harrington are my friends. They have had a terrible experience here in Marseille," Fatima told her cousins. "They need our help. And these are my cousins, Amal and Maryam," Fatima announced.

Gabriel and Finley greeted the young women politely, then waited. After a brief indecipherable discussion, it appeared Amal had asked the guard to fetch her father.

Assad Al Aziz arrived within minutes. He was the antithesis of the cruel Arab sheikhs portrayed in European literature and art. He was a cheerful Turk, a short, stocky little man with a twinkle in his eye. He had a loud laugh that rolled out of his rotund little body and carried over the water.

The patriarch stepped forward and shook Gabriel's hand and then Finley's.

"Welcome, welcome," he said jovially. "I believe that you have been victims of a terrible crime. I hope that we can make you comfortable and that you can end your day on a good note."

"Thank you for your kindness," said Gabriel.

"My daughters tell me that you are looking for a vessel to take you to the Black Sea. Is that correct?"

"Yes, sir," answered Gabriel.

"Are you travelling to the Black Sea by yourself?"

"No, sir. I was appointed to see Miss Harrington safely to Constantinople. After our disastrous first day here, I feel it is my duty to stay with her for the full duration of the voyage. Miss Harrington is determined to reach the Crimea."

"It is a wise decision to accompany her. I don't understand why the young women of today want to be so independent. I have a lot of trouble with my daughters," he added with a chuckle.

"Is she a nurse? A lot of them have passed through this port."

"No, she's looking for her father. We were attacked by a thief and thus didn't we board on time. Our original plan was to sail directly for Constantinople. Now, we need a new plan."

"Then, Mr Craddick, you must come aboard immediately, and we will plot a course for you."

Assad ordered the guard to assist them with their luggage.

"Join me," Assad told Gabriel, and the two men walked away, leaving the women behind them.

"You are an Irishman?"

"Yes, Sir. To be sure," he added with a twinkle.

"Your nation is close to my heart."

"As is mine to yours. We have a remarkable history between our countries."

"What is your business in Constantinople?" asked Assad.

"I am writing a book, and I would like to write it in that city. Your country saved a lot of people from starvation in my hometown, Drogheda."

"That's an interesting story."

"I don't live in Ireland anymore. Switzerland is my new home. Geneva."

"Aha!" exclaimed Assad with delight. "Is it as beautiful as they say?"

"More so," Gabriel smiled.

"Why did you leave The Emerald Isle?" asked Assad.

"I lost my family. I lost everything. There was nothing left for me. I wanted a new beginning in a new country."

Discussing his past with Assad gave him a heavy heart, and he hoped that the man wouldn't press him for details.

"The young lady you are escorting—".

Assad paused.

"—Are you in love with her?"

"Oh, bloody hell, no. Whirling dervishes cause less chaos around them," Gabriel blurted out. " I'll do what Mr Hudson asked of me, and that'll be the end of it. Finished."

Assad had not expected that answer, and he laughed. If his belly weren't so round, it would have been folded double. His entire body shook with mirth.

"There are many miles ahead of you, Gabriel," he laughed. "Don't say no just yet."

*

Amal and Maryam were enjoying their visitor, even though she could hardly talk. They had settled her on their father's private deck and made her as comfortable as they could. Finley sat in the fading sun, enjoying the fresh air and a clearer mind.

After fetching freshly brewed tea for their patient, they let it cool a little, then laced it with mint, pine nuts and a lot of sugar. They fed her tiny spoonful's of the mixture. Finley was adamant she didn't want to eat, too exhausted and achy from the abuse that she had suffered earlier. Her head wound was tender, and she dreaded seeing her black-and-blue face staring back at her from the looking glass. Taking out the small bottle of Fatima's tincture, she had two drops. It began to ease the pain but did nothing for the exhaustion.

*

Amal and Maryam began to chatter like two birds.

"Mr Craddick is so handsome. You are lucky to have him as a guide," said Maryam, the more outspoken of the two sisters.

When they saw that Finley couldn't, or wouldn't, answer them, they changed the subject.

"We are from Constantinople. My father is a liberal man. He insisted that we be tutored in English. We have an Irish governess. We are likely to attend university in Germany since they are open to the idea of educating women. It is our father's dream that our country becomes modern and can build relationships with Europe. He is a peaceful man, and he wishes that the Ottoman Empire will come to peace with its neighbours," said Amal. "War is a frightful thing."

The girls continued to jabber away without noticing Finley, who didn't really care by that point, had dozed off.

*

After some time, Gabriel Craddick appeared on deck and wondered about Finley's whereabouts. He saw her reclining in a soft chair, fast asleep. The sisters had covered her with a soft blanket to keep her toasty. Walking across the deck, hands in pockets, he dropped to his haunches when he reached the girl. He studied her bruised face while Maryam spoke to him.

"She drank tea, Mr Craddick," said Maryam, "but she didn't want to eat anything."

"Is she speaking yet?"

"No, Sir, she is very tired."

"Will there be space for her in the woman's quarters?"

Despite his irritation with the defiant girl, Gabriel would gladly have sacrificed his bed for her, mainly because Samuel and Assad would have expected it.

"There is always space for visitors," smiled Maryam, who used the opportunity to study the rugged Irishman. One day she wanted a husband that looked just like Craddick. Even by eastern standards, he qualified as a very handsome man.

*

They left Gabriel alone with Finley. He stared at her for a long time. He moved his hand over hers and gently pressed it. She was in a sorry state, and he felt guilty that he had been so hard on her. She was attacked was because she fought to reclaim his case. A case he was careless to lose.

"Hello, Miss Harrington," he whispered. "I came to see if you got yourself into any more trouble while I was away."

Finley opened her eyes, small slits in a bruised face.

"You must rest. Amal and Maryam will take care of you."

Gabriel thought he saw a small nod.

"Assad Al Aziz can take us as far as Malta."

"When?" she whispered.

"Midnight."

This time she nodded properly.

"How long will it take?"

"Two days if the wind blows in the correct direction, and the gods are with us."

Finley was too tired to respond beyond a croak. He inched closer to her and touched her wound gingerly. She flinched.

"You still have an almighty big bump. We must keep it clean," he said with a frown.

He gently pushed Finley's hair off her forehead.

"You will feel better in the morning, I promise."

"Mmm," was the only sound that Finley could muster.

"You are very brave, but you must promise that you will never do that again."

"Mmm."

"Thank you for saving my suitcase. There are important documents in it."

Finley whispered something that he couldn't hear.

He stroked her hair softly and shushed her. His emotions were a muddled mess of guilt, primal urge, kindness, and loneliness. He was sure every fibre of his being told him to kiss her. It was the closest that he had been to a woman in ten years. Confused and defensive, he decided to ignore any more silly suggestions from his brain and promptly moved out of the danger zone.

*

Amal and Maryam took her by the armpits and lifted her up. Finley's wobbly legs tottered uselessly beneath her as the two women negotiated the route down to her cabin, then they helped her get dressed for bed.

When they examined her bruised head and face closely, they were surprised she had survived such a severe blow. With her hands and face washed, Maryam dug around in her suitcase to find a nightdress.

"You only have men's garments in here," she complained.

It was only when Amal tossed everything out of the case that she found Fatima's donated kaftan. Maryam gently pulled it over Finley's head as Amal held her arms aloft.

The cabin was warm, lined with layer upon layer of colourful, thick Persian carpets of all colours and sizes. Even the walls were covered. In the middle of the room sat a squat beaten copper table with cedarwood legs, surrounded by a selection of luxurious cushions. The large four-poster bed carved out of rich teak supported the softest down-filled mattress that Finley had ever slept on.

Amal and Maryam helped her to bed, pulling the thick silk sheets and eiderdown over her broken body. Before they could blow out the oil lamp, Finley was asleep.

12

THE KINDNESS OF STRANGERS

There was nothing humble about Assad Al Aziz's sailboat. The dhow was a floating palace disguised as a ship. The women's quarters where Finley was hosted were extravagant. The women didn't wear burkas or hajibs in those areas, which meant Finley had time to study Amal and Maryam in daylight. The sisters were fascinated with her hair, admiring the long strands of straight blonde silk that hung to her waist. In turn, Finley couldn't stop admiring their exotic features. Sensual and feminine, they moved with grace and dignity. Their faces were warm and friendly, and they smiled readily. Finley was touched by their kindness. She would never experience that level of hospitality in her own country.

Faiza Bdra Al-Fahrat, the girl's mother, was a majestic woman. Nobody could doubt her gravitas as the matriarch. Assad had never taken and the second wife because Faiza had threatened to kill him if he did. Being a modern man, Assad took the threat seriously. She had negotiated with him on behalf of her unborn daughters before she married him, making him promise that they would be educated.

Further, there would be no arranged marriages and no second wives. Their girls wouldn't live like ghosts in the back of the house. Assad promised Faiza everything, and he had never failed on that promise.

Faiza was intimidating but also kind and welcoming. She was stern but showed respect to her servants. She never raised her voice, and in return, they would do anything she asked them to,

"Do you always sail with your father?" Finley asked Amal a few days later.

"My father is a trader," answered Amal. "Sometimes, the routes that he sails are dangerous. That is when he forces us to stay at home."

"We can't always leave Constantinople. Sometimes we have to attend our lessons," Maryam complained.

"But soon," Amal trilled, "father is taking us to Venice to watch a famous opera. We will be staying in a grand hotel."

"Will you cover yourself when you are at the theatre?" asked Finley.

"Certainly not," interrupted Faiza, passion in her voice. "We will dress modestly. That is enough. When in Rome, I say. Assad will understand. I'll make sure of it."

The three young women giggled and grinned.

"My father is also a liberal man," answered Finley. "He has allowed me to do everything that my brothers do."

"Brothers? Tell me about them," Faiza said.

"Yes, I have four. We are a close-knit bunch most of the time. We love each other very much."

"Love is a sign that you have very good parents."

The smile on Finley's puffy face evaporated.

"Mother died when I was four years old."

"That is sad. I am sorry for you, my dear."

"Where are your brothers? Why are they not with you on your quest to find your father?"

"I ran away." Finley quipped with a smile. "They would have tried to stop me if they knew my intentions."

"And this man you are travelling with, Mr Craddick. Is he an honourable man?"

"Yes, I believe that he is," replied Finley, "As the only girl in our household, I am versed in observing men and judging their motivation. Mr Craddick is a good man but difficult. Distant when it suits him. I don't fear him, although he has a bad temper when things don't go his way."

Having seen Gabriel tend to Finley as she dozed, Amal wanted to intervene—but she kept quiet. To her mind, he was neither difficult nor distant. She had seen a kind, compassionate man. The Arab girl wondered what had happened to Gabriel. *'Why does he insist on scaring people away to protect his heart?'*

*

Exhausted with all the chatter, Finley fell asleep on the soft bed.

"Let us leave her. She is a brave young lady
wanting to travel to a theatre of war. She needs
rest. Her head wound must heal quickly. I think
her time with us will be her only moment of
solace in the weeks to come."

*

Finley slept most of the day and woke up at twilight. Gathered on the cushions around the small table, the women dined together. The fayre was fragrant and exotic, served with the fresh flatbreads Finley loved. The standard of living on board the ship was overwhelming. Even better than her family home at times. The sense of peace and well-being as the dhow cut through the waves made her wonder if she could live on a boat all year round.

"Mama says that you need new clothes," said
Amal. "Something more lady-like for you. She
thought it would cheer you up. Come on, let us
see what we can find in our wardrobes."

Maryam did a jig on the spot with excitement until Finley declined the offer.

"I can't travel in a lot of clothes. I can wear your
clothes while we are at sea, but I am facing a
Russian winter. I only have my small case with
me, and I need to keep warm."

"But—"

A servant interrupted Maryam.

"Mr Craddick has sent a message asking Miss Harrington to meet him on deck."

Finley washed and put on the latest set of contributed clothes, then limped upstairs, with Faiza two paces behind planned to catch the girl if she tumbled.

*

As she emerged on deck, Gabriel's back was to her as he stood watching the glistening water. A tunic hung untidily over his trousers. His hands were in his pockets, and his black hair was pushed back out of his face by the wind. It was twilight, and the moon was rising. The dhow's sails caught the wind efficiently, and the angular hull sliced into the waves effortlessly. Craddick heard something behind him, then turned to see a brave-faced Finley walking towards him, teeth gritted, smile forced. Despite the pain, she found it a pleasure to breathe the fresh sea air after recuperating below deck all day.

Finley's pretty peacock-blue kaftan, embroidered with gold, silver and blue thread, fluttered around her. A flowing scarf covering her hair—and the wound—gently flapped in the breeze.

Gabriel frowned when he saw her. It was the first time she had worn something ladylike in front of him. The garment was wide, but when the breeze clamped it to her hips, it could no longer disguise the tempting shape of her body. They had been together for three days, and this was the first time that he paid attention to her. Even with her bruised face, she was lovely.

"Hello, Finley."

She gave him a slight smile.

"You look a lot better than when I left you last night."

"Yes, they have looked after me well. I am overwhelmed by their hospitality."

"The Turks are a cruel but generous nation," Gabriel commented cryptically.

"Why do you say that?"

Gabriel ignored the question and continued on a different tack.

"We reach Malta tomorrow. Assad has invited us to accompany his family to the opera in Venice."

"No!" Finley said emphatically.

Her body stiffened with rage as she expected Gabriel to disagree with her. She prepared herself for an argument.

"I agree. I have told him that we need to reach Balaclava as soon as possible."

"Mr Hudson said that you would only take me as far as Constantinople," she corrected.

"I am fully aware of the agreement. I have simply invoked one of the special clauses."

"And?"

Gabriel reached out and drew her closer to him. He gently cupped her swollen face in his hands.

"I will never forgive myself if something happens to you."

He found himself staring into her eyes—but it was to be a fleeting moment of tenderness. Once Gabriel realised what he was doing, he pulled his hands away abruptly. Feeling uncomfortable, he shoved them deep into his pockets and turned his back on her once more.

"Go on, go to bed. Get some rest."

He made sure that she was safely below deck before he went to his cabin. There, he felt the memory of her soft skin against his palm all night.

13

WHY?

There was a quiet knock on the door. Finley stood up to answer it, but before she could cross the room, Amal and Maryam had let themselves in and smiled at her.

"May we?" asked Amal, who carried a pot of tea and tasty treats.

"Yes, of course. That looks delicious."

The girls sat on the large cushions and drank tea around the low table.

"This is delightful," said Finley biting into a tasty treat flavoured with rose water and nuts.

"When do you eat this?" asked Finley.

"Every day, and at festivals," laughed Maryam.

"Festivals?" asked Finley.

"Yes, Eid-al-Adah, Eid-al-Fitr and many others."

"We know that the Christians have a holiday soon," said Amal.

"Yes," smiled Finley, "on the twenty-fifth of December. Christmas."

Finley became pensive as she dwelled on the yuletide season, remembering how her father would take her hand when they went to church. When her tiny hand slid into that big warm palm, and she felt safe. She wondered if she'd ever feel his hands again but quickly dismissed the thought, not wanting a shred of pessimism to take root in her. That would help no one.

"What do you do on that day?" asked Amal.

"We eat a lot," laughed Finley. "We had a cook called Bella who made so many mince pies, I couldn't count them all. They are sweet treats as delicious as these."

The words took her back to the kitchen at home. It had a wooden floor made of oak and a long rectory table that stretched down the middle. Bella would knead the pastry while Finley assisted her in filling the tiny pies with the most delectable stewed mixture of raisins and currents. She remembered the heart-warming aroma of them baking. Bella would hand her one, still warm from the oven, and pour her a glass of milk.

"On Christmas Eve, our family would gather in the parlour," explained Finley. "My mother always made the room look beautiful. She would drape long strands of holly and mistletoe. Wreaths made of prickly holly with its shiny red berries were hung on all the house's doors. My mama did it all by herself. She did it for us children. My father was not often at home, off on a tour of duty. It was very special when he was with us."

She had a vague memory of her mother. It was blurred and far away. Yet, every time she thought about it, she felt the magical atmosphere of that special Christmas Eve. Finley and her brothers sat in the parlour in the dark, except for the soft candlelight. Emma lifted Finley onto her knee as they sat on the red velvet sofa. It was warm and soothing and made her drowsy. Her playful brothers would squash onto the sofa, too, all trying to be close to Emma. She would tell them the story of Jesus's birth.

All Finley could remember after that was her father bending over and kissing her mother. The kiss lingered, making an impression on her young mind. She decided mama and papa loved each other, and she felt safe. Finley never saw her parents kiss each other again. She couldn't remember anything else about that Christmas, yet she would always remember the kiss. She had never experienced the warmth of Christmas that way again, but she would associate Christmas Eve and candlelight with love for the rest of her life.

The church was always lit with candles and mistletoe. In the corner stood a nativity scene. The Virgin Mary was always dressed in blue, and the shepherds looked poor and scruffy. The parishioners always put hay into the crib to make it look real. Mary, Joseph, and baby always had yellow halos painted on their heads, and Finley thought they would have looked better without them.

Music soared through the church as the congregation sang 'Silent Night', 'The First Noel', and Finley's favourite, 'Oh Holy Night'. The music would touch her spirit and as she became older. It would move her to tears. The sheer magnificence of hundreds of voices in unison would surely reach the heart of God.

The wise men were the most intriguing. Her father told her that they were kings from the ancient worlds. She had forgotten the names of those countries. Christmas was always a simple family day with no fuss. Colonel Harrington refused to have any ostentatious guests.

Suddenly, she felt homesick.

"Why is this man Jesus so important?" asked Amal.

Finley pondered the question. There were many answers, but she wanted to explain it simply.

"He was very important."

Finley paused

"—God sent Himself to give us hope."

It had been a long but pleasant chat. Seeing Finley's eyelids drooping, Amal and Maryam said goodnight. The girl climbed into the warm bed, but she couldn't sleep. Eventually, she fell into a restless doze. She dreamed about her father. He was tired and bloodied, and he was reaching out to her. No matter how hard she tried to run to him, she couldn't. She was paralysed. His image began to fade, and she shouted for him to come back. Finley woke up screaming, her heart beating, her brow beaded with sweat.

14

PORT VALLETTA

They moored in the Maltese port of Valletta just before sunset. With its magnificent lateen sails at a jaunty angle, the dhow stood in stark contrast to the tall British Naval ships reaching directly for the sky.

Assad and his family stood on the wharf, bidding farewell to their guests.

"I hope to see you in Constantinople, my friend," said Assad.

" I look forward to meeting once more," Gabriel said sincerely, clasping the man's hand firmly.

They all said goodbye to each other with words of thanks, blessings, and long life. Faiza watched the two travellers walk away. Gabriel was charming, albeit in a moody manner. He was a commanding figure, a leader. He'd make an excellent husband. Finley followed him, clad in layers of winter clothing. She was tenacious and determined. The partnership would never be without conflict, which was a good thing. Faiza had foresight, and her sixth sense told her that they would marry.

*

It was raining, and the water had pooled along the wharf. Gabriel and Finley sloshed through the puddles until they

---

found the old steps that led them up to the city. Everything around them was a visual delight, especially the baroque architecture. From the great fortifications, they overlooked the harbour. The sky changed from orange to violet, and finally, the sun set peacefully in the west. Their boots were soaked, so they went in search of a place to sleep for the night. They weren't fussy. All they wanted was a warm room with a fire where they could hang their boots to dry.

"We will find a cheap place for the night. Look for the word 'locanda'," he told her.

They walked through the wet streets, and Finley saw the sign first.

"There," she pointed.

The exterior of the building was stone. The arched door was battered by the elements and neglect. They would have missed it except for Finley's keen eye. They opened the door and waited in the courtyard. Within seconds, a dainty Italian man appeared out of nowhere. He was small, flamboyant, and as dramatic as his British clients would tolerate.

"Bouna serato, Signor. Benvenuto."

"Good evening," growled Gabriel.

"How can I help you, Sir?" the owner asked in broken English.

"I need a room where I can dry out," said Gabriel.

"Si, si. Capisco. There is only one room left on the third floor. Is that accettibile for your *moglie— er—wife*?"

Finley tried to object, but Gabriel took her hand and squeezed it gently, followed by a look that said, 'keep quiet.'

"Yes, that will do," answered Gabriel.

"Your name?"

"Mr and Mrs Craddick."

Finley made no comment. Gabriel held her hand until he picked up their suitcases. The concierge observed the girl's clothes which he thought were hideous. Later, he would enjoy a little wine and tell his friends that he had met an English woman who was extremely beautiful but had no sense of style whatsoever. Her husband was stunningly handsome, but she looked like a pirate.

*

The lodge was larger than it appeared on the outside but just as run down. A large sun-bleached carpet lay over the stone floor. There were remnants of ancient murals, but the walls were damp, and the paint had peeled off. The furniture was ornate but ill-kempt. The upholstery on them was old and worn through to the wood. The staircase was made of ebony, which had been shipped from the far east to Malta, but the timber was dull and lifeless. It had not been oiled in years.

Finley stepped into the room where they would sleep for the night. A match spluttered as Gabriel struck it to light a single oil lamp. The bed had meagre coverings, thoroughly unsuitable for winter. It was pushed up against a peeling wall. A large cupboard was squashed against the bed, and a dusty chandelier hung from the raw wooden beams above.

Finley wondered if the chandelier had ever been lit or cleaned, for that matter. Other than that, there was nothing in the room, not even a carpet.

Gabriel lit the fire, and the room gradually warmed up. They both took off their boots and hung them to dry in front of the fire. Finley climbed onto the lumpy mattress because she had nowhere else to sit but the cold floor. He kept brushing up the cinders in the hearth to keep busy.

"Come here, for goodness' sake. Stop sweeping up nothing. You need the rest. I have four brothers. We often shared."

"If you insist," Gabriel said with a smile.

Tentatively, he walked across the room and made himself almost comfortable, sitting upright against the creaky old headboard.

"This room is sparse," Finley chuckled.

"It's not the worst that I have ever lived in. For some, this would be a palace."

"Where do you come from?" asked Finley.

"Drogheda, Ireland."

"Do you still live there?"

"I live in Geneva."

"Why there?"

"They have a neutrality policy. I have seen enough death and violence. I want to live as peacefully as I can."

Faiza had packed them a fine meal in some waxed paper. Finley unwrapped it on the bed.

"This looks nice," she said, smoothing out the wrapper to form a makeshift tray.

A feast was piled on the paper. Faiza had included some of the flatbread that Finley loved combined with a rich mixture of currents, raisins, and cheese.

Opening the other parcel, she chuckled when she found a small bottle of wine, rather than the orange juice she had been expecting.

They ate together in silence.

Gabriel shuffled to the end of the bed and took his notebook out of his case, pulled the lamp closer to him, and began to write. He was pensive and distant. Finley studied his facial expressions. Sometimes, he would frown, smile, or even laugh. At other times he would stop and just stare as if watching a scene from long ago. His scribbling was agitated. Sometimes, he held his breath and pushed down upon the pencil with such force that she was sure that he would break the lead. He seemed to become more troubled until he threw the pencil down, fell back onto the pillows and stared at the ceiling.

"What are you remembering that is so painful?"

"Nothing," lied Gabriel, "I am just frustrated."

Finley went to her suitcase and took out Fatima's kaftan. She opened the cupboard and used the door as a screen. Gabriel turned away, walked to the window, and looked at the street below, trying to ignore the fact that a beautiful woman was undressing behind him.

Seeing the reflection, Gabriel turned around in the split second that Finley slipped the kaftan over her head, giving him a clear view of her long legs and firm body. He quickly turned back.

"Have you ever been in love?" Gabriel blurted out.

He had no idea why he asked her the question. Perhaps it was the wine? He leaned against the wall, watching her, arms crossed.

"I don't think so," she answered honestly. "Why do you ask?"

"I don't know," he shrugged.

Gabriel knew exactly why he asked. He wanted to know if she had someone in her life or if she had ever been hurt. He was not usually inquisitive about a woman, but Finley intrigued him. She was young, beautiful, and brave, with brief moments of vulnerability. She made him laugh, and he was beginning to enjoy her company.

"Are you afraid of me?" he asked her.

"Not at all."

"There is only one bed in here."

"We can share it," she smiled.

"I don't know if I want to be in the same bed as you."

His mind snapped back to the kaftan wafting down her lithe body.

"You can relax, Gabriel," she said with a wink. "I promise that you are safe with me."

He looked at her and laughed delightedly.

"Thank you," he said with a broad smile. "I was worried that I would have to spend the night on the floor."

She fell asleep immediately, but Gabriel remained awake for a long time. He looked at Finley, aware of his proximity to her. When he did doze off, he dreamt of his wife, Shauna.

*

Gabriel knew that it was morning, but he didn't want to let go of the dream that he was in. He was aware of someone beside him. He put out his hand, and he touched Finley's flesh. His soul soared. All the horrors of years past had been a terrible nightmare, and Shauna was still next to him. He felt joy that he had not felt for years. He put his hand out. He felt the curve of her body under the bedclothes. His groggy eyes expected to look into hers, soft and green. But it was not Shauna. It was Finley. He spiralled into the darkest place his tortured mind had ever taken him. His soul was as black as night. He felt the pain of disappointment and sorrow all over again. The longing for his wife ate at his core. Sleep had played a cruel, evil trick upon him. Shauna was dead. She would never return. Never!

Gabriel was struggling to navigate back from his nightmarish dreams to reality. Rage boiled up from his belly and tingled in his clenched fists. He looked at Finley's serene face. It was not her fault that he had experienced the forbidding dream. He didn't know why, but he bent down and kissed her forehead softly. She continued to slumber. Knowing that he was at a crossroads, the choice was stark. He could live in the past forever or find a reason to live for the future.

*

Gabriel wanted to get away from the small inn and leave the morning horror behind him. He woke Finley.

> "Come on, it's time for us to find that ship bound for Constantinople."

They slipped out of the battered door onto the cobbled streets and walked in the general direction of the steps that would take them to the harbour.

It was warmer, and it had stopped raining. It seemed that there was something especially important happening on the streets of Valetta. The place was teeming with people wherever she looked.

> "It is beautiful," she said. "What are they doing?"

The citizens of Valetta were using a great amount of imagination and creativity to replicate their ideas of Christ's birth in a host of nativity dioramas. Some scenes were sophisticated, others were humble. The materials varied too. Some were made from finely carved wood, others old rags, branches, pinecones, whatever people saw fit to convey the story.

"They are beginning to prepare for the eighth of December. They start weeks in advance," Gabriel told Finley.

"What does that mean?" asked Finley as they walked along.

"It's the day of the 'Immaculata'. The day of the Immaculate Conception. They will put nativity scenes all over the city."

"How do you know?"

"I am an Irish Catholic," he smiled, "This is the tradition. Christmas celebrations begin on this day and end on the 6th of January."

"Where are the Christmas trees?" asked Finley.

"They are only popular in England."

"And Germany," Finley frowned.

"Yes," said Gabriel.

"I recall that we never had trees as small children, only when Eleanor came into our lives, desperate to look ahead of the times. How do they celebrate for a whole month?"

"Like everybody else who is festive. They eat, go to church, midnight mass, sing carols. The children have processions through the streets and perform plays. Interestingly, a young child gives the church sermon on Christmas morning."

"Why is there no baby in the manger?" asked Finley.

"They only put him in on Christmas day."

"We have lost the essence of Christmas in England. For the poor, it is just another day, and for the rich, it is about showing off. Do they celebrate Christmas like this in Ireland?" asked Finley, curious to hear more.

"Some people do."

"And you?" asked Finley.

"I never celebrate Christmas ostentatiously," he answered casually. "I see the holiday differently."

"How is that?"

"It is a time to be with people you love."

Finley wanted to ask more questions, but the shutters had dropped over his eyes, and he seemed to take on a dark mood. She was sorry that she upset him, but it was not deliberate. She didn't know what she had said that was offensive, but something had irritated him.

They walked in silence for a while, and when they reached the town square, Gabriel's mood began to lighten.

*

Gabriel took her to a small coffee house that read *Caffé Cordina*. Like everything else in Malta, the tatty exterior belied the fine interior. The maître d' gave Gabriel a long critical stare. When he had the cheek to ask for a table, the man took one look at Finley's attire, and his British snobbery overcame him.

"No!" he declared, his nose wrinkled as if he was smelling something foul. Pointing outside, he added, "We only have tables on the pavement."

Craddick's black Irish temper got the better of him, and he grabbed the man by the collar and pulled him across his desk until their noses were touching.

"I want a table inside, or I'll break yer bloody legs, so I will."

Gabriel shoved the stuffy man back to his side of the desk. His menacing tone was all the incentive the waiter needed to improve his manners. The Englishman rearranged his collar and politely showed them to a table, acting as if nothing was amiss.

"You're grumpy," she teased, hoping to ease the mood.

"I bloody well am, yes. And I am hungry too," he complained.

Gabriel and Finley didn't talk to each other until their breakfast arrived. They looked over the water, each harbouring their own thoughts. Finley picked up a discarded newspaper and flicked through it, looking for any information from the war office. The sun broke through the clouds, and it baked down upon the ancient city. The port was full of naval ships from Britain, France, the Ottoman Empire, and Sardinia. It was sad to be reminded of war in such a beautiful place.

"We have to get rid of these suitcases," said Gabriel, "I hate the bloody things. They are awkward. I am not carrying this thing all the way to Scutari."

"Do you know if we can sail directly to Constantinople from here?" asked Finley.

"I would say yes, but I can't promise."

"How many days will it take?"

"Perhaps five if the gods are with us."

"They were last time," smiled Finley.

"The weather is going to change. Prepare for it. This is our last port of call until we reach Asia. Buy whatever you need to. Don't get caught out."

"What do we need?"

"Warmer underclothes, preferably wool. That fur you brought was a clever idea. Our coats will not keep us dry. We need mackintoshes, lined leather gloves. An 'uhlan', a woollen mask that covers your face. The Polish soldiers wear them against the cold."

"Socks?" Finley asked.

"Newspaper and socks. You can even put newspaper into your trouser legs if you are desperate. It is the best insulation that you will ever use."

"Where will we pack the new clothes?"

"Something called a knapsack. You wear it on your back. Frees up your hands a treat."

"Where will we find these items. There are no suppliers here."

"We will get them from the army stores."

"How? We don't know anyone there."

"You can buy anything for the right price," said Gabriel.

15

BOARDING THE STEAMSHIP

After finding a rogue quartermaster who helped them acquire the goods they required for two tins of baccy, Gabriel and Finley stood in the port. Now, they needed to find a ship that was sailing to the Black Sea without stopping along the way.

"Ideally, we want a passage on a private steamship," he told her.

Finley nodded, and her eyes began to scour the quay. A steamer was docked between the British Fleet, and it had no naval insignia on it. Gabriel headed over. Finley waited. She was obvious in the sea of white uniforms, and Finley Harrington didn't want to bump into anyone who knew her father. Anthony Logan was a case in point.

The newspaper mentioned had Logan had fled to Malta to escape the scandal he had caused in London. For the establishment, his dishonourable conduct with a fellow officer's wife had been deeply embarrassing. It was the ultimate betrayal of a brother-in-arms and a great humiliation for the government. After the article about the Paxton Party appeared in The Times, the general was summoned by his superiors. Instructions to leave England immediately were given. It was excellent news for General Logan, who knew that although there would be some gossip in Valletta, he wouldn't be regarded as the town idiot, as he had come to be known in London. Relieved, he accepted his orders gracefully and boarded a ship to Malta that very afternoon.

Days before, he had received a letter from Eleanor pleading with him to take her to some South American destination where they would be anonymous, and could both live out his twilight years pretending to be important.

His superiors made it clear to him that his career was over, and as soon as the war in the Crimea ended, he would be expected to retire with dignity and honour. He would be given a jolly good send-off and would receive a pension for the rest of his life.

If it were up to the military, he would have been allowed to stay, but alas, the politicians were demanding his head. General Logan was both furious and embarrassed. His introspection was limited, and he lay the blame firmly on the shoulders of The Times. He refused to acknowledge that it was his beefy hand clenching the luscious breast of Mrs Harrington.

As he walked down the jetty with Admiral Maddison, he saw a woman standing alone on the wharf. There was something familiar about her, and as he got closer, his irritation piqued. He had only met her once, and she had made a lasting impression upon him—a bad one. She had belittled him, and he had vowed to take vengeance. He had spent many nights plotting her downfall. She was tall, slim, and graceful. Her golden hair was blowing in the wind, her eyes were the colour of the sea, and she had the confidence and tenacity of Miss Nightingale.

Thankfully, Finley had not been in London during the furore, but if had she been, he would have ignored her
completely for fear of embarrassment. For a moment, he
stood and admired her as a woman, then his mind was cast
back to the day that she had made him look like a fool. He
watched as a rugged ill-kempt man approached her. They
began to talk to each other in earnest and seemed to be in
deep conversation.

Gabriel and Finley were too distracted to see the general
sauntering toward them. The admiral had left General Logan alone on the wharf, finding something more important
to do than entertain the disgraced military man.

"Good day, Miss Harrington," said Logan, almost
standing on top of her.

For a moment, Finley was confused, then realised who it
was. She didn't greet him but nodded her head, which annoyed the general no end. Gabriel noted the cool exchange
between the two but said nothing. General Logan looked
the Irishman up and down and decided that he looked like
a hooligan.

"Who are you?" he asked Gabriel disrespectfully.

"Gabriel Craddick."

"An Irishman?"

Gabriel ignored the remark, but the general wanted to
make a point.

"That explains your slovenly dress."

Gabriel didn't respond but sunk his hands into his pockets,
a subtle gesture of his contempt. The general was used to

men jumping to attention when he spoke. This Irishman didn't. The general directed his next question at Finley.

"What brings you into my harbour?"

"It is none of your business," she snapped, looked him in the eye.

"I can have you court marshalled for your insolence."

"On what authority? I am not in Her Majesty's army."

Gabriel watched the exchange, wondering what the relationship was between the general and Finley. Logan had not approached her out of kindness or curiosity. He had a card to play, and he knew that it would torment her.

"I have news of your dear, papa," smirked the general, sarcasm dripping from every word he said.

Finley's eyes lit up with hope. She couldn't have wished for a better surprise. It was remarkable. Even if the words were coming out of the despicable fellow's mouth.

"Is he alive?" she asked hopefully.

"I am sorry, my dear," he said in a smarmy tone. "I can only give that news to the next of kin, his wife. We have tried to reach her, but we can't find her."

Finley felt rage building in her chest, but she controlled herself. She didn't want the general to gain pleasure from her disappointment. Gabriel had not said a word. He knew the general had the power to put him in gaol if he set one foot wrong. It was more important that he and Finley reach the Black Sea than brawl on the quay with this loathsome specimen. For an Irishman, there would be no reprieve.

"My brother Lester stands proxy for my father when he is away or in the event of something happening to him," Finley told him coolly.

"Since you are here, it may be a very long time before they can provide you with the evidence that we have," he smirked.

It was the mocking smile that turned Finley's internal fury into physical violence. She was tall, lithe, and strong. Her brothers had taught her how to protect herself, so she knew how to box. If she could take control of a thundering horse, she could stand her ground against a fat, ageing general.

Finley changed her stance and balled her right hand into a tight fist. Turning her torso, she yanked back her arm as far as it could go and bent it in line with her shoulder. The sucker punch landed between the ogre's eyes, just as her brothers had taught her. Gabriel was shocked. It was an almighty blow. He had never seen a man throw such a perfect punch, let alone one a woman. The general staggered backwards dizzily and crashed to the ground, landing on his backside. Gabriel knew that the man would have two black eyes the following day and that he would probably have to bandage Finley's hand. He prayed that it was not broken.

Soldiers and sailors flocked to the general's aid, but he shouted for them to leave him alone. He could have charged Finley with assault, but he knew he would look like a fool standing in court looking like a panda. It would create an even greater scandal if The Times found out that he had been beaten up by a girl on his own naval base wharf. He tried to get up with dignity but failed, rocking back and forth on his haunches. A kindly sailor helped him up, but as soon as he was standing, he shoved the man aside. He longed to retaliate and threaten Finley with her father's life, but he could feel blood clouding his eyes, and he knew that if she hit him again, he would need the infirmary.

Finley was not finished with Logan. The man was puffing and panting like a small steam engine when she grabbed him by his khaki tie.

"Where is my father? Tell me, or I will beat you back onto your arse as quick as a flash, and you will be even more of a laughing stock at this base."

Gabriel was becoming anxious. Finley was creating a stir, and he wanted to flee Valletta. She was courting trouble, and he couldn't protect her from the consequences.

Finally, the general came to his senses.

"We had a letter from the hospital in Scutari. He is there."

*

Gabriel grabbed Finley by the arm, briskly marched her toward the Sardinian steamship and pushed her up the gangway. As soon as they were out of sight, Finley snatched her hand to her chest, and tears welled up in her eyes.

"It hurts so badly!"

"I know. It's happened to me before. Let me see it."

She gave him her hand. It lay limply in Gabriel's warm palm. The sensation reminded her of her father. He examined her hand but didn't touch it. Her fingers were swollen and already turning blue.

"Can you move your fingers?" he asked.

"A little."

"Let's hope that you didn't break your hand. It would be a disaster."

They felt the steamship begin to move. In the chaos of the moment, they had forgotten where they were.

"Do you think the general was telling the truth?"

"I don't know," said Gabriel.

"How can we be sure that my father is in Scutari? What if Logan lied?"

"We'll only know when we get there, Fin."

Gabriel pulled a tattered tunic out of his knapsack, tore it into strips and began to bandage Finley's hand firmly.

"Where did you learn to fight like that?"

"My brothers taught me," she laughed, despite the pain.

"They did a decent job. I'll have to be careful of them."

Her smile as she remembered them was bittersweet.

"It's a relief to know that you can look after yourself. I eat my words. You don't need me to protect you, Finley Harrington."

"Perhaps, it's just good to have you with me."

Finley didn't know why she said it. It was a slip of the tongue. He didn't see her blushing, but he did hear what she said as he finished dressing another of her wounds.

*

Later that evening, the Italian owner of the lodge met the British maître d' at a little tavern in town.

"I met the cowboy and his wife this morning," said the Englishman.

"Well, what did you think?"

"You were right, Giuseppe. Mr Craddick is the most handsome brute to visit this island in years. I would love to get to know him."

"Do you think that he is approachable?"

"But, of course, he is," laughed the maître d. "Which self-respecting man would want to be seen with a woman like that? "

"They are married," protested the Italian, making the sign of the cross.

"Well, who of us is not?" said the Brit. "I must get home to Marjorie before she begins to worry about me."

*

As the steamer sailed eastwards, the weather became cooler. They sat on the deck. Finley filled the time watching Gabriel writing. He felt more than saw that she was restless.

Are you bored?" he asked.

"Yes, I am."

Gabriel stood up and went to their cabin. He came back a few minutes later and threw a book at her. She caught it effortlessly.

"Read it."

She browsed the cover.

"I have read it, thank you."

Gabriel looked at her in surprise.

"What do you think of him?"

"It's his first book. Tolstoy is going to be the finest modern writer to come out of Russia."

Gabriel cocked his head and studied her.

"You surprise me all the time."

"My father may be a soldier, but he is educated and so are his children."

Gabriel sat down next to her and looked out to sea, lost in the moment.

"What made you write?" she asked.

"The suffering I watched around me."

"I am sorry."

"I want to tell my truth. Nobody has to agree. I am not here to convert the lost. I just tell stories from my perspective."

"You are successful. I see your books everywhere."

"I am contentious, not successful."

"What are you busy with now?"

"A truth that will shock Britain and set me free."

"What's it about?"

Gabriel Craddick shook his head. He couldn't tell her. He couldn't bear his soul, except on paper. He stared at the horizon, seeking solace in the beauty of the harsh sea. He was slowly dying. His anger, bitterness and hatred were killing him. He prayed that the book he was writing would be cathartic, but instead, it was destructive. He was opening doors that should have been left firmly locked and never opened again. Unable to rid himself of the grief of the past, he was convinced he was cursed.

16

THE STORM

Making steady progress, the ship would be in the Aegean Sea within a few days, leaving the Mediterranean behind them. On reaching the Dardanelles, the vessel was to continue through the Marmara until Constantinople. From there began the final short, overland leg of the route to Scutari.

Gabriel was terrified of what Finley might discover when she arrived at the hospital, and he didn't know how to prepare her for the worst. Finley was in her early twenties and idealistic. At that age, he thought he could conquer the world too.

Finley lay in the dark cabin. It was the only vacant space on the vessel. All the other places were crammed with politicians and engineers. It was large, with two comfortable bunks on either side and a desk between them. Gabriel and Finley were travelling under the same surname. Anything else would have created a social uproar on the ship.

Finley, dressed warmly and smothered in layers of bedclothes, looked like a small creature hibernating. Gabriel, with other plans, had found conversation and a bottle of whiskey in the mess with the officers.

Finley must have dozed off because she heard the cabin door smash open when Gabriel returned. The whiskey had got the better of him, and his sea legs failed. She watched him undressing clumsily in the dark. He was trying not to wake her but crashed around, having the opposite effect.

Although he was only a shadow in the dark, she could see his outline, his well-defined muscular back, neck and shoulders, his wavy hair that curled in the nape of his neck. Finley had the desire to reach out and run her fingers through it.

Hidden in the dark, he continued to disrobe until he was naked. He was stunning. Feeling voyeuristic, she was embarrassed by her thoughts. She closed her eyes, hoping that he would be dressed in his nightshirt when she reopened them. She heard him clamber into his bunk. There was no noise after that. He fell asleep immediately.

*

Within hours it was bitterly cold. The temperature had plummeted to near freezing. Finley woke up shivering and forced herself to get out of bed and put on extra layers. She moved about, looking for the coat, trying to be quiet.

"What's wrong?" asked a drowsy voice.

"I am freezing."

"Come here. There is space for both of us. We will warm each other. It will only become colder."

"I will be warm in the fur," she muttered.

"Alright," he mumbled, turned around and went back to sleep.

Finley covered herself with more even layers. She crawled back into her bunk, trying to keep the sheets still to retain what little body heat they held. It was futile, her body temperature had dropped, and she was cold to the core. There was no tea or hot water available. In the middle of the night, she doubted that there was anyone in the galley to help her. Her teeth began to chatter, and she had to force her jaws together to stop them. Her nose felt like a chunk of ice, and it began to run. Soon, her whole body was shivering continuously.

It was then she gave up and pushed the blankets aside. Her joints were stiff from the cold, and it was an effort to get up and negotiate the few steps to Gabriel's bunk. She removed the heavy coats and crawled into his bed, then pushed her body up against him, desperate to absorb all the warmth she could. She began to thaw. Her blood began to flow through her veins, and within a short while, she was warm.

Gabriel felt the girl climb into the bunk, and after some time, she stopped shivering. She was welded to him perfectly, and he could feel every curve of her body coupled with his. They fit together perfectly. It was as if they were one.

A dashing man, in the past, Craddick had many admirers. Some of the women he met yearned for permanent love. Others were happy with a brief encounter. Although he declined all the offers, he was filled with temptation. The idea of lovemaking with this woman filled him with fear—the fear that he might enjoy it. Gabriel couldn't sleep the rest of the night, torn between dread and desire.

Dawn arrived abruptly with the weak winter light trickling through the porthole. Finley had tossed and turned in her sleep until she lay in the crook of his arm with her head on his shoulder. Her skin was flawless, her hair draped over his arm, and her sensual tawny lips turned up slightly at the corners. After much deliberation, he decided he liked having this beautiful woman in his arms, shielding her with his body. It was uplifting to feel human touch once more. After that, he wasn't sure. He did know he felt content in the moment. He wanted to savour the intimate experience, not moving for fear that she would awaken and leave. For the first time in years, he had considered a physical bond with someone who wasn't his wife.

One thing he was sure of was that this young woman had come into his life and turned everything upside down. His mind was travelling to places he had not dared to consider for years. What if he made a mistake? He found some solace by remembering his promise to Sam Hudson.

"She's a capable young woman, Gabriel. Take her as far as Constantinople. She'll find her way from there. She is a colonel's daughter. The army will look after her."

Then, he remembered watching her sleeping figure on the train to Marseille, looking like a Nordic goddess in the moonlight. His mind changed tack yet again. *'Be honest, Gabriel. You know you could never abandon Finley. You should take her Scutari, and perhaps further if she wishes.'*

*

Finley awoke with Gabriel watching her. She noted he was frowning as if pondering a question.

"It was very cold. And you did offer? Don't you remember?" she said quickly.

"Indeed, I do," he said with a smile. "And it was a very good idea. You'd have been a block of ice by now."

"Did I wake you up with my fidgeting?" she asked

"Not at all," he lied. "I sleep like the dead."

Laying in the crook of his arm, she realised she had never been as intimate with anyone as she was at that moment. Every nerve in her body was alive, reacting to every movement that he made. She looked into his eyes. They were gentle this morning, a window on his soul. He was the man that she wanted. Finley had finally met the man for whom she had waited. Confused, she chastised herself for reading romance into what was purely survival. *'The feelings aren't true, Finley Harrington. They were born out of desperation.'*

Gabriel had been able to turn his back on a lot of women, but he didn't want to turn away from Finley. The longer the situation went on, the more he knew that it was time to confront the pain and the fear of the past and put it behind him. Gabriel didn't give his mind time to thrust itself back into the past. Boldly, he pulled Finley towards him and kissed her. The kiss was hungry, passionate, and determined. It was everything that Finley wanted but nothing that she had expected.

*

The wind became fiercer, and the gale was escalating. It didn't take long for the Aegean to be whipped into a frenzy of salt and foam. The waves rose higher, and the troughs sunk deeper. The skipper dropped the sails to save the masts and gain better control of the ship. The stokers shovelled mountains of coal into the massive boiler engines that were fighting to propel the ship forward. For the crew, the pressure grew. If the engines stalled, the vessel would be unable to navigate the waves. If hit at the wrong angle, the ship would cartwheel to the bottom of the ocean, just one of many. The Aegean Sea was usually tranquil, but now the elements were at war. It was a miracle that the boat was still afloat.

*

Gabriel and Finley stayed huddled together in the cabin at the centre of the boat in a failed attempt to find some stability. The couple sat on the floor and wedged themselves between the bunks, the only way to prevent being tossed around. Gabriel stowed the loose items under the bunks to protect them.

Finley watched the porthole dip beneath the water. She was terrified. For all her travelling experience, she'd never experienced a storm of such magnitude. All that she could think of was the cabin flooding and them drowning.

"I can't stay in here," she yelled above the noise, "It's suffocating. I need air."

Finley stood up and ran toward the door. Her legs were uncertain, and she was thrown across the cabin as the boat crashed into a trough. Gabriel stood up. He was also off-balance, and he grabbed Finley by the arm. They stumbled backwards, hitting the wall of the cabin as the ship rose.

"We are going to drown," screamed Finley.

"No, we are not," shouted Gabriel above the noise. "Sit down. Please?"

"The ship is going to sink. We are going to die."

Her eyes were big and startled. Secretly, Gabriel empathised. It was the worst storm that he'd ever experienced—and he was well travelled.

"I want to get out," cried Finley.

"Finley, stop it," he shouted at her, but it made no difference.

Gabriel pulled Finley toward him and cupped her face in his hands.

"Look at me, Fin. Look at me."

He held her head firmly and forced her to comply.

"If you go onto that deck, you are as good as dead. A wave will wash you off, and that will be that."

Gabriel grabbed her and crushed her to his chest.

"Yes, that's better," he said, caressing her hair to make her give up on the idea. "Are you warm enough?"

He felt her nod.

"Close your eyes. I will look after you."

The ship climbed a swell and fell about twenty feet. Their bodies took jarring blows every time it happened, but he didn't let her go. Trying to distract herself, her thoughts turned to happier times at home with her father and brothers.

"Do you think that we will live to see Christmas?" she asked him tearfully.

'Of all the questions in the world, why did she ask me that one.' Catapulted into the past with such violence, he couldn't think clearly. It was the worst question at the worst time. His eyes teared up as the agonising memories tore through his mind. Finley felt his arms clench around her.

*

It took an entire day and night, but the storm finally abated. They dragged themselves up from their hiding place. Their cold, exhausted bodies ached. Now, there was no storm to distract them. With some effort, Gabriel and Finley climbed onto his bunk and covered themselves with every garment and quilt that they could muster. His arms went around her again, and he looked into her eyes. They lay together quietly for some time.

"Fin, I promise you that you will see Christmas. After everything that we have been through so far, this storm is just a day at the races."

He gave Finley such a charming smile her heart soared. Staring into his eyes, she tried to speak. She wanted to tell him that she loved him. But how could she be in love with somebody she had only known for a few days?

"Gabriel— she began.

Before she could finish, he kissed her. First gently, and then more eagerly. Finley pulled away from him, still trying to tell him something.

"I know what you want to say, Fin, but this is not the right time. Not tonight."

Finley tried to interrupt him, but he clapped his hand over her mouth.

"Don't argue, Finley. Don't protest," he said fiercely. "You don't have a choice. Erase any thoughts of another man. I am yours. But you will wait for me. There are things I need to finish. You must trust me. There will be a time for us. I will marry you, and I will never leave you for as long as I live."

Finley saw the familiar fire in his eyes and the passion in his voice. She was clamped in his embrace. There was no talk of love, only Gabriel's command to wait.

17

THE KEY TO WAR

The steamship progressed well. The tempestuous seas had calmed, but the further east they sailed, the colder it became. The misty drizzle was continuous. The captain of the ship assured them that they would reach Constantinople by the morrow.

"We are preparing to sail through the Dardanelles. We travelled faster than we anticipated," he told Gabriel. "After the storm, the wind turned, and the powerful current pushed us forward. We sailed at twice the knots we would have with just the engine, and we gained time. It may have been terrifying, but it hastened the voyage."

"Every sacrifice has a blessing," Gabriel noted with a smile.

"Once we dock in Constantinople, our mandate is to despatch this cargo as soon as possible."

"How bad is it? What can we expect when we reach Scutari?" asked Gabriel.

"I have seen many wars, but this one is different. It is savage, and the casualties run high. The guns and cannons are powerful. They boom out across the landscape. The army engineers have built railways, and there are new systems of communication. Truthfully, it is a slaughter, exacerbated by the superiority of the weapons they manufacture. This is the worst situation that I have ever seen."

Gabriel could only nod.

"You said earlier that you are a writer. What do you write about?"

"I try and tell the world about the futile horror that people inflict upon each other."

"Then you write about war."

"War is not the only horror that people suffer. I write about disease, famine, poverty, slavery."

"Do you sell many books?"

"Yes."

"Promoting harmony must make you popular?"

"Good grief, no!" he chuckled. "Mostly, I am unpopular. I ask awkward questions others shy away from. I try to make people think."

"How so?"

"Well, take governments as an example. It is easier to make war than to make peace."

"That's an interesting statement," the captain said, brow furrowed.

"Russia stepped back months ago and evacuated the area. The war could have ended then were it not for the politicians. Why is that, captain?" Gabriel asked rhetorically. "Do you believe it is cowardly to be a man of peace?

"No. It takes a remarkable amount of courage to follow the path of a good man."

Gabriel smiled.

"Why are you on this journey to Constantinople, Mr Craddick?"

"Because The Ottoman Empire helped my people, and I want to tell the world the story. I believed that Constantinople would be the best place to pen it. Alas, I was asked to escort the lady. She has taken up a lot of my time."

"I can understand why," chuckled the old sea dog. "She is exceptionally beautiful."

"Her soldier father is missing, and she was determined to find him," Gabriel told the old captain, ignoring the man's observation.

"If she was prepared to travel to hell to find her father, what would she do for her husband?"

"That's a poetic way of seeing it," Gabriel said, followed by an awkward grin.

"So, you do have feelings for Miss Harrington?"

"You've turned into a gossiping housewife, skipper," the Irishman joked, embarrassed.

The gnarled old captain clapped Gabriel on the shoulder while giving him fatherly counsel.

"Fate has brought her to you, Mr Craddick. Don't waste an opportunity to fall in love."

*

As the ship sailed, Finley stood on deck, covered from head to toe in an attempt to stave off the cold. She stared across the snow-covered land, Gallipoli to the north and Ottoman Anatolia to the south. The Dardanelles Strait was a narrow but crowded ribbon of water, a major shipping lane. Small ice mounds drifted on the water, which the larger ships pushed aside. The smaller boats had no option but to navigate around them. Although there were countless ships, sailors and passengers around her, loneliness engulfed her.

Seeking solace, she went to the galley to find a cup of hot tea.

"My pleasure, Miss Harrington. I shall bring it to your cabin, yes?"

"Lovely, thank you."

Back in their berth, she sat down in front of Gabriel. He seemed emotional and distant. Tormented, his one hand had bunched into a fist, and the one tapped the table. The pencil lay in the middle as if it were flung there. His brow was furrowed, and his eyes were squeezed shut. But it wasn't writing the book that was the problem this time. It was simply the last few lines. The final words choked him. He felt sharing them would be a betrayal.

"There is only one way for me to end this book, but I can't."

"What stops you?" asked Finley.

"Guilt," he stated.

"Guilt?"

"Yes, Finley. Guilt."

"What have you done that you can't forgive yourself?"

Gabriel was tired, confused, and irritable. He was wrestling with himself. Frustrated, he slammed the book shut.

"Here, take it."

He slid the book across the desk at her.

"Find out for yourself. One day you will read it anyway. Today's as good as any other."

"You have written many things, Gabriel. Why is this book so difficult for you?"

"It's a confession."

Her fingers traced down to the middle of the cover, and she opened it. The writing looked like bitter scratches across the pages as if the paper didn't want to accept the truth. Her eyes scanned the title.

"Is this your life up until today?"

"Read it. Just bloody read it."

She looked at him, hurt and angry.

"No, I won't! I wouldn't want to intrude on your precious privacy. If you want me to know what it says, you'll have to read it to me."

"Why must you be so damned difficult?"

"Because I am your friend, not your editor!"

Gabriel dropped his head and rubbed his eyes. There was silence between them for an hour. Only the howl of the wind could be heard. Eventually, he began to speak in his beautiful, lilting, Irish accent.

"The Ships of Drogheda, by Gabriel Craddick"

18

GABRIEL

Gabriel Craddick sat on his pony and looked into the lush valley below. For one so young, he was observant, astute, and critical. His governess, Miss Richards, regularly accused him of asking questions well beyond his age. He was a sensitive boy but wild and spirited. Where he had learnt empathy and kindness was a mystery. It was not from his parents.

He looked at the tenant's cottages, scattered amongst the picturesque scene, little white blocks, surrounded by patches of brown, in a sea of green. From a distance, they were pretty, thatched dwellings. Close up, the picture was different.

Men were busy tending the fields, and the womenfolk were washing clothing and cooking on open fires. The laundry hung over the wooden fences, and the colours made the scene below particularly cheerful. There were plenty of children dotted about as they earned their keep. Working beside their parents, the boys tilled the soil, and the girls cooked and cleaned. There were a few carts shared between the community rather than having a particular owner.

The children were supposed to attend school, but Gabriel never saw any one child attend five days in a row. They took turns, and when it rained, they all stayed at home.

They were very lucky—it seemed like it rained almost every day in Ireland.

He spied on what they were doing for a good while, and then one day, he plucked up the courage to go down into the valley. At first, he stood under a tree and just observed them. When the villagers started a game of hurling, they spotted him. They called him over to join in. For the first time in his young life, Gabriel Craddick made friends.

He could hear laughter and cajoling. On Saturday, they played traditional Gaelic tunes. Some were melancholic, others loud and raucous. The musicians' fiddles and the whistles would echo through the valley as the onlookers sang and clapped their hands to the music. It was then, Gabriel watched people dance for the first time.

The people in the valley would also drink ale they brewed from barley and yeast. The thick black liquid, decanted into large barrels, quickly hidden from view. Beer was more likely to be stolen than money. Whiskey was poured straight. It was a staple that saw them through the harsh winter nights and replenished their humour and personalities, which they lost struggling in the miserable cold. It was this aromatic spirit that made all the tenants hooligans. Some became happy hooligans, others horrid.

Life was difficult for the tenants in the valley, but the Irish were social creatures by nature, and the merriment made life bearable. That was until the fun and laughter reached Bill Craddick's ears. He couldn't bear the sound of happiness, and he used to send his men to shut them up.

*

The Craddick's house loomed over the valley, large, immaculate, and comfortable. The family was not as well off as the local English gentry who surrounded them, but they were rich. Gabriel's father regularly told people how he had built the farm from scratch with his bare hands. But that was not so. Billy Craddick had inherited a small piece of land from his father and expanded it by gobbling up every piece of land around him. If someone became bankrupt, he would buy it at the auction because it was cheaper. He bought arid land, rocky outcrops, marshes, and vacant plots, but mostly tenants' land after they were evicted.

Gabriel's mother had given birth to him in her later years, and by that age, his father had no desire or care to raise a child or celebrate a son, not even his first. Gabriel was nurtured by a wet nurse, raised by the kitchen staff, taught by a governess, and when he reached the mature age of eight years old, he was posted off to a boarding school. His parents didn't accompany him. He was taken to his new school by Miss Richards.

> "You will do well here, Gabriel. You aren't a
> hooligan. Soon, everybody will understand you as
> I do."

Gabriel only had one sibling, a sister, Anette. She was older than him by ten years, and she could barely tolerate the lad. Gabriel never behaved like other children from elite families. She tried to avoid him. Gabriel knew intuitively that Anette was a nasty person, and it gave him an intense pleasure to get her riled, particularly if she had company.

Gabriel was mostly left to his own devices, which was the only plausible reason for his happiness. He had intellect and a grand sense of humour which was accompanied by resilience. It was a rare combination in wealthy offspring.

Gabriel endeared himself to the tenants who lived in the valley below. He could never understand why some people were rich, and some people were poor. There was so much of everything. He annoyed his parents no end with his charitable ideas.

When he came home for the holidays, he would rush down to the valley to participate in the chaos of everyday life and the simplicity of the ordinary folk. They laughed, danced, told old stories. Of course, they drank and beat each other as well, but their lives were honest and authentic. It was simple. He knew his friends, and he avoided his enemies. He felt no desire to be in the large sterile house where his mother pretended to be gentrified.

On his return for the Christmas holidays, Gabriel had his first brush with injustice when he was twelve. It was a severe winter. The frozen ground made life difficult. He empathised with the villagers who found that fuel for their fires was in short supply. He walked along with the men, gathering anything that could be burnt for heat. The food they saved would only last the winter, and they prayed that the spring would arrive on time so that they could plant a crop as soon as possible.

Two days before Christmas, he begged his sister Anette to part with some clothing for the tenants.

> "Anette, you don't wear all of those dresses or coats. People are freezing to death. They don't have shoes."

Desperate to help them, Gabriel always pestered her friends in the same way. Anette would die with shame.

She slammed open the cupboard door, annoyed that Gabriel was forcing her to do what her servant usually would. Anette grabbed every irreparable garment in her cupboard, the dresses with the biggest stains, the largest moth holes, the frayed hems. She threw them at his feet, one by one, spitting 'take them to the dregs', her terminology for the tenants.

Something about that word 'dregs' jarred in Gabriel's soul, and he felt anger rise in his chest. It was that word, on that day, at that moment that extinguished any affection he may have felt for his sister, which wasn't much. He didn't understand what he was feeling, too young to identify righteousness.

It was Christmas Eve. The house was busy. Servants and cooks were preparing for the evening celebrations. The Craddick's had a reputation for providing the most lavish meals of the season. Delightful smells emanated through the house, and Gabriel sat in the kitchen drinking tea and eating a mince pie.

His mother, Colleen, ventured into the kitchen, which was unusual for her. Anette was prone to tantrums, and to keep the peace, her mother had lowered herself all the way to the laundry.

"Come here," she pointed to a young laundry maid. "Miss Anette is looking for a particular dress, have you seen it? The blue one."

The young servant was terrified of the mistress of the house.

"I seen it on some girl in the vall—" stammered
the girl.

"No, mother," Gabriel interrupted. "Anette gave it
away. I delivered it."

All eyes were upon mother and son. The boy had been forthright, and there were witnesses.

"Don't undermine me when I am talking to the
servants, Gabriel."

"But mother! Anette gave the dress away to
charity."

Colleen Craddick looked down her nose at her annoying and outspoken son. She wished she had never conceived him. He was a blemish on her near-perfect life.

On Christmas Eve, Colleen successfully combined an atmosphere of eastern magic and Christian holiness. The Craddick family and their guests departed thirty minutes before midnight to attend the mass. Hundreds of candles were lit. There was a beautiful display of the nativity scene, and the sound of Christmas carols echoed in the old church. It was a spectacular show, orchestrated by a spectacular cast. There were no poor tenants at the glorious event. They were attending a different mass, not two hundred yards away, in the remnants of an old chapel with old, battered pews. Colleen would have insisted they choose another god if she had the power to do so.

When they returned home in the early hours of Christmas morning, as Mrs Craddick was undressing, she mentioned the episode of the dress to her husband.

"We must keep the tenant farmers under control with firm discipline," said Bill Craddick. "I will make no exceptions at Christmas. I will take the young lady in hand tomorrow. Don't let it spoil your day."

*

Billy Craddick was away at first light. He barged into the laundry and ordered the young laundry maid to the stable. Then he ordered the stableman to fetch the girl who was accused of stealing Anette's dress. Billy Craddick waited impatiently. He was wasting precious time on Christmas morning.

From his lonely bedroom window, Gabriel saw Mr O'Dowd return with young Katy Jones, just turned sixteen.

"Is this the girl who stole the dress?" Bill demanded.

"I don't know if it was stolen Sir, I only recognise the dress."

"Remove your dress."

Mr O'Dowd was appalled. The old man knew what was coming and turned away but forced himself to stay in the barn. He knew that Bill Craddick would violate Katy if he was left alone with her.

"Does your family need food?" Billy Craddick bellowed at the poor waif. "I will turf them off their land before the day is over if you don't obey me."

Katy knew that Mr Craddick would do just that. She slowly began to undress until she stood in her undergarments, almost naked.

"And the rest."

Peering around the stable door, a young Gabriel felt bitterly sorry for Katy, and he was appalled that his father made Katy remove her clothes in front of him.

"Father! Stop, please!" He begged. "Don't hurt her. Please don't hurt her. I can explain everything. Anette gave me the dress. She knew I took all the old clothes to the valley."

His father looked at him coldly. Never wanting the boy in the first place, all he wanted was to beat the spirit out of him.

"Is there a witness, boy?" he snarled, spittle flying.

"Yes, father, but Anette is still asleep. I will fetch her."

"We will not wake Anette for a matter this trivial. I shall deal with it here and now."

"But father, I took the dress. I gave it to them."

"So, you are both thieves! Collaborators. Let me show you what I do to thieves in my house," he shouted, his eyes were filled with evil intent.

Billy Craddick, a powerful brute, grabbed Gabriel by his shirt front. His boy tried to wriggle from his grip, enraging the man even further. He threw his son to the ground with all his might.

"Give me the whip," he shouted at the stableman.

"Now, Sir, let's think about this. It's Christmas day. A time of peace. Just hear the boy out."

"Don't tell me what to do, O'Dowd! Give it to me, or I will evict you right now. Let this be a lesson to you as well."

With a bowed head, O'Dowd passed the whip.

Billy Craddick began with Gabriel and didn't stop beating him until the seat of his pants was a pulp of wool and blood. The lad screamed constantly as his father whipped him, but Billy Craddick showed no mercy. Tears streamed down O'Dowd's face. When Billy Craddick was satisfied that it was a job well done, he picked up his son like a sack of grain and slung him into a corner.

Stripped bare, stood clutching her arms to protect her modesty, Katy was dragged over next. Secretly, the sight of her nakedness aroused Billy more than the thought of the violence to come. The first crack of the whip against her pure white skin was the only sound. In defiance, Katy bit her lip and clamped her eyelids shut. At the corner of her eyes, tears weaselled their way out, dripping on the floor. Her agonised silence frustrated him, so the brute thrashed the girl until she began screaming for mercy. When she collapsed, he was still not satisfied. His hatred for the girl couldn't be satiated, even when the welts on her back oozed out rivers of blood.

Through his pain, Gabriel watched a sinister grin develop on his father's face. *'He's a monster.'* The terrified lad saw Katy sink to the ground. He got up and charged at his father. Bill Craddick grabbed his son by the hair and pulled the boy up until he stood on his tiptoes.

> "I want you at the table by noon. You will not
> mention a word of this to anyone. And you will
> show no hints of pain."

Gabriel spat at his father. The spittle ran down Billy Craddick's forehead and into his eye.

> "I hate you, father. I will never sit at your table,
> even if you beat me to death."

Billy Craddick would have gladly killed his insolent son that day, but his wife interrupted him. An important visitor had joined the family for Christmas luncheon.

> "Billy, where the devil are you? Father Augustus
> has been here half an hour!"

Colleen Craddick stomped into the barn and saw Gabriel and Katy, battered and bruised. The sight meant nothing.

> "Mr O'Dowd, burn that rag," she snarled, pointing
> at Katy's dress on the dirty floor.

Colleen Craddick turned to her husband, doing her best to ignore the blood splatters adorning his shirt.

"That's where you are. Hurry up. We don't want
to keep Father Augustus waiting."

She said nothing to her son. He may as well have been invisible.

*

As the dress burned in a brazier, Mr O'Dowd had the wisdom to put Katy, and Gabriel, onto a cart and trundle down
to the valley. Katy lay on her side, barely conscious. Gabriel
cradled her head on his lap. He looked down to brush her
hair from her face. Looking up at him was a pair of google-
eyes, leaving only the whites visible.

The mood was gloomy. O'Dowd's depressed head lolled,
the stableman barely looking where he was going. The one
day a year that these humble families could be together had
turned into a tragedy before the day had even begun. Katy's
mother wept, and nothing could console her. Her father
stood beside the cart, defeated and humiliated. Feeling his
age after years of hard graft on the land, his fighting years
were over. His gaze fell to the frosty ground, his eyes glazed
over with shame. Weary old men and women observed
with sad eyes, and a pall of silence hung over the valley.

The young men were filled with fury, ready to risk everything for justice. The young women were afraid, trying to
talk sense into their vigilante husbands' heads.

"You will hang if you touch Bill Craddick. You
know how it works for people like us."

It was the mothers in the small community who were fearless. Mrs Jones was no different. She lay her precious
daughter on a kitchen table and cleaned her wounds with

salt water. Other women were kind enough to do the same with Gabriel, the son of the monster who had flayed the girl. Seeing some concerned women peering in from outside, Mrs Jones gave them a task too.

"Bridget, Cissy, Connie. Fetch the constabulary."

They would be gone a while, their destination three miles away. The womenfolk left behind began to pray.

Katy Jones died on Christmas night, just moments after the constables arrived. The two policemen looked at the bludgeoned girl. It was too much for the younger, inexperienced officer. The gruesome sight forced him to flee outside to wretch.

Katy's young man, Liam Ryan, looked down at his sweetheart. He had never seen her naked before, and he wept openly. She had been innocent and chaste. Billy Craddick had stolen his happiness.

Without anyone noticing, he marched to the Craddick house and asked to see the master. Billy Craddick was good and drunk, and he sauntered into the courtyard leaning heavily on a walking stick. His belly was fat and full, and his cheeks looked rosy.

"What is it?" he barked.

"Katy," was the only word that Liam could get out.

"Who?"

"Katy Jones," said Liam.

Billy Craddick laughed.

"Didn't I teach her a lesson! I whipped that seductive lily-white flesh in fine style, didn't I? As a good Catholic boy, I bet you've never seen all of her womanly charms, eh?" Craddick goaded. "But I have. Every inch of her and every time you look at those curves of hers, you can think of me."

Liam Ryan didn't give any thought to what he was going to do. He simply lashed out with the axe. It hit Billy Craddick's fingers, gripping the walking stick. Four sausages fell to the ground. Liam stumbled backwards, startled by what he had done.

"Get off my land!" bellowed Billy, too drunk to notice the amputations.

It was only when Colleen came to call him back to the dinner table that the gentleman of the house realised he was injured.

The women of the valley marched behind the constables, all the way to the big house. There, the officers arrested Billy Craddick and Liam Ryan.

*

Two days later, Billy appeared in court. If he had been poor, he deserved the death sentence. If he weren't surrounded by guards, the mob would have murdered him. The judge understood the privileged man's predicament. In fact, everyone understood it, because they had similar problems. Craddick's legal counsel said, 'servants steal, tenants steal, everybody steals.' Many heads in the room nodded.

"Billy Craddick couldn't allow theft under his roof. He was well within his legal rights to whip a

tenant or a servant for any transgressions. It was
an accident that the girl died. Witnesses said she
must have hit her head when she passed out,
drunk from the night before. That was the true
cause of death."

The judge had to think carefully, and with the help and influence of the local gentry, he made a ruling.

"Billy Craddick, you are an educated man, rich in
skills. Now, you are an invalid, losing the four
fingers off his right hand."

In his mind, the judge felt that the injury was punishment enough. It was a shame to hang a fellow with such talent. The judge had two options for Billy Craddick. He could be executed, or the rogue could dedicate his life to Her Majesty's army.

Major Billy Craddick, his wife and daughter, were welcomed to India by the Commissioner.

Liam Ryan was deported to Australia and sentenced to serve fifteen years of hard labour.

*

Gabriel didn't go with his family, and they didn't care. He was as good as his word. He never sat at his father's table again. Colleen and Billy Craddick were satisfied with the rumour that he was living in the valley. It was sufficient evidence that he was alive. Anette met a British officer from an influential family. They married one year after she arrived in India.

The tenants in the valley were left to mourn the death of Katy Jones. The only proof that she had been there was a tiny mound of earth in a sea of emerald grass. On top of it was a small cross, carved from local stone, with her name on it.

Katy was just another sacrifice to the ancient god of greed.

19

INJUSTICE

Finley wept. She wept for Katy, Liam and all the tenants in the valley. She couldn't stop. She stood up and walked around the cabin, tears running down her face. It broke her heart. Gabriel fetched tea, and she tried to gain her composure.

"Did you ever see your parents again?"

"Never."

"What happened after that?"

"I stayed there. You could say the tenants adopted me."

He stopped for a while.

"How did you fend for yourself?"

"I worked like every other boy of my age did."

"Did your parents leave you any money?"

"No, and even at the tender age of twelve, I would never have taken it. It was blood money," said Gabriel.

"And the house?"

"It was sold to another miserable tyrant, Sir Gerald Shaw. But he was not as bad as my father was."

"Were you happy with the villagers?" asked Finley.

"Yes."

"How did you adapt to life in the valley?"

"At that age, it was a wonderful adventure, a new world. I loved the idea of sleeping up in the hayloft with all the other chaps. We worked extremely hard. Made mischief. I laughed more than I ever would have in my father's house. It is terrible to be poor, Finley, but other things make life rich."

Finley nodded, prompting him to continue.

"I learnt the value of a warm bed after a chilly day. Planting seeds and seeing the first leaves emerge. Eating food that I grew. Laughter. The warmth of a conversation at the end of the day. "

"Who took you in?"

"Fergus and Maeve O'Donnell. They had a cartload of children," he laughed. "They didn't bat an eye at taking me in."

"Did you go to school?"

Gabriel chuckled softly.

"We were little ruffians. Father Vincent was the local priest and teacher. He was relieved when we didn't show up for lessons. He was a young man and out of his depth with us. The government insisted we attend, but I would have rather put in a full day's work than go to school. Thankfully, I had been at boarding school and had some years of basic education."

Finley smiled.

"There is an honesty about poor people. If they steal food, it is because they are starving, not for any selfish or insubordinate reason. Rich people will take the food out of a poor man's mouth purely because they can."

Gabriel was intensely emotional.

"They did precisely that just ten years ago and continue the same practice today. The poor were starving, and instead of feeding them from the bounty the Irish harvested, they took the food away on great ships. It was preferable to make money than show mercy and feed the starving masses. The poor man who dies of starvation because of the wealthy man's greed—that for me is murder."

The depth of Gabriel's feelings and thoughts were making an impact upon her. The way he spoke allowed her to experience the world as he had.

"How did Father Vincent convince you to write?"

"It wasn't him that compelled me. It was Maeve, Fergus, and the boys. It began by me telling a story, which became a tradition."

"Which story?" Finley frowned.

"It was my job to tell the Christmas story every year and to make it interesting."

"I am sure you succeeded."

"Indeed, I did."

*

Maeve and Fergus O'Donnell sat on the only two chairs that they owned. Their nine children sat on the floor around them, ten if you included Gabriel. They had finished a dinner of potato, carrot, and bone broth. It was Gabriel's favourite meal, and to date, he had never met anyone who could make it like Mrs O'Donell. Maeve had the creativity to create a feast with three ingredients. They ate out of tin bowls and ate with wooden spoons carved by Fergus himself.

It was Christmas Eve. They had spent the day doing all the usual things that needed tending to. The animals had to be fed and watered. Fields needed to be weeded. Two boys were sent off to find some honey. But the next day was Christmas, which meant special food. Maeve had saved for a cut of meat. It was a tough cut, with a lot of bone and gristle, but she had a knack for cooking it. There was also plum pudding. In the dead of winter, how she found the plums was a miraculous mystery.

Fergus and Maeve weren't ardent fans of attending church. Fergus complained that he couldn't afford to tithe, and he was going to hell anyway. Maeve supported Fergus on his refusal to take the family to church. Her philosophy was, 'my soul is my own business.'

The small kitchen was teeming with children, and Maeve was becoming short-tempered. Fergus had a few pints in his belly, and he had no concern over what the little blighters were up to.

"Get ye up oota that chair, Fergus O'Donnell and take the strap to these louts," cried Maeve.

"It's Christmas Eve, Maeve. Put yer rolling pin away, lass."

"Christmas Eve, yer say, you could'na remember the story of Christmas for yer life."

"That is why we had the bairns, Maeve, so they can remember what we forget."

Fergus O'Donnell rolled with laughter. Even after a tankard or three, Fergus stayed kind. He could have a laugh at everything. Eventually, he convinced Maeve to have a tipple with him. From there on, it was each man for himself. As soon as Maeve and Fergus were jolly and distracted, the little O'Donnells used the opportunity to participate in the golden nectar as well. This year, Maeve would have none of it, and she watched them like hawks.

"Get outta that barrel, yer louts," she yelled. "Get over there on the floor by yer father. He has a story for you."

"Aw, feck, Maeve. It's been years."

"Then use one of 'em bairns you have been talking about," Maeve ordered.

Fergus O'Donnell, stumped for a suitable tale, wasted half an hour on some ancient game of elimination until the person picked to tell the story was chosen fairly. Gabriel was that person, and he had to tell the story of the nativity.

"Just don't tell it like Father Vincent does," shouted Fergus. "We want an interesting story."

All the children yelled in agreement, and Gabriel was put under pressure to create an epic.

"Once upon a time," began Gabriel.

"Naaaaaah," the children roared, "that's what Father Vincent always says. It's boring."

After several false starts, his audience was satisfied. Gabriel told the story in a manner that they had never heard before.

*

Gabriel's sat in the firelight. His eyes became distant and dreamy. He was no longer in the cottage. He was standing on the hills overlooking Bethlehem.

He began to paint a picture with his words. His audience was mesmerised. Nobody moved as the young lad shared his epic interpretation of the tale. Fergus didn't even raise his hand to drink his ale.

"It was winter in Judea. The air was dry and crisp, and the city stood in a stony landscape. The Roman soldiers stood guard at the city gates. The city was congested with people returning to their hometown to be counted. Outside of the walls were large caravans and tents of all shapes and sizes. As twilight set in, lamps and fires began to twinkle on the desert floor like fireflies on a summer evening."

The storyteller looked at the open mouths around him then continued.

"The horizon was spectacular with bands of colour, from orange to violet fading slowly into black. Against the silhouette, a man leading a donkey and upon it was a young woman. As the couple drew closer, everybody saw that the woman was with child and close to giving birth."

"Then what," Maeve mouthed, hanging on his words.

By the end of the night, the O'Donnell family could see the baby Jesus in the manger. The light of Christ illuminated the room, and it penetrated their hearts, bringing peace beyond understanding.

An unusual quiet calm hung over the cottage for the first time in the history of the O'Donnell family. They drank tea on Christmas Eve instead of beer. Maeve had made biscuits. The family sat around the fire quaffing the hot, sweet brew, chomping on ginger snaps.

"Tell us the story again," nagged young Joey.

The cottage was small, and the family was poor, yet that Christmas eve, as they had huddled together in front of the fire, Gabriel decided he was going to be a storyteller for the rest of his life.

Later, Maeve and Fergus climbed into their narrow cot.

"It's the best Christmas Eve I have ever had," said Fergus, "no matter how poor we are, Maeve, tonight there is peace and love in this house."

*

Word travelled, and soon Gabriel gained a reputation for telling stories. He never ran out of ideas, and he was sought after in the pubs and inns as a narrator. One afternoon, Father Vincent arrived in the O'Connell's yard. He had given up on the O'Connells coming to mass or contributing to the parish. Every O'Connell had disappeared when he reached the cottage, and Gabriel was left to face the priest.

"I don't want anything from you," said Father Vincent.

"Yes, Father," said Gabriel.

The cleric pulled out a leather-bound book and a pencil.

"You are never at school, so I don't know if you can read or write."

"I can, Father."

"Very well, lad. Take this."

He shoved the book and pencil into Gabriel's hands. "Write down your stories, son. One day the entire world will read your books."

"Thank you, Father."

Gabriel looked down at the slim little notebook and turned it over, again and again in his hands. Within minutes he knew what he would write about.

Father Vincent never visited the O'Connell family again. He knew when he was defeated. Gabriel would see him in town from time to time. He would tip his cap and greet him politely, but they never spoke. Many years later, long after Gabriel had left Ireland, the old priest was walking through London. He stopped at a bookshop and looked through the tiny window. There was a book on display, authored by Gabriel Craddick. The old man smiled to himself, strode inside and promptly bought it. He opened the book. There was a dedication:

> 'To Father Vincent of Drogheda, who made me a writer.'

Finley smiled at Gabriel.

"He was a kind man."

"Yes, his kindness shaped my life."

*

Gabriel was not sure how the next chapter in his life would affect Finley. Rather than words, there was a nervous cough.

> "She was young and sweet. Only a slip of a girl. There were a lot of girls in Drogheda, but I had never paid much attention to women. Pa always teased me that I should have joined the clergy."

It was high summer. The air was fresh that night, and it was dry. Gabriel sat in Mulligan's bar drinking an ale before he began his story for the evening. Struggling to count the people, it was the largest group who had ever come to listen to him. Paddy Mulligan told him to sit on the bar counter, in full view of the punters. He needed no notes. Gabriel's story was written in his mind, and he had gone over it a thousand times.

He studied the audience. These were the people that he loved. They sat on benches, drinking beer and whiskey. A rusty violin creaked somewhere, and he heard someone yell for it to shut up. In the far corner, squashed between her mother and father, was a girl he had never seen before. She had the face of an angel, pure innocence. For the rest of the night, he couldn't keep his eyes off her. He was riveted, and everybody faded away. The lass was the only person in the room for Gabriel, and the story was just for her.

Gabriel didn't realise how overt his reaction was until the next day when word went around the raconteur was in love with Shauna.

> "He didn't take his eyes off her," said Maeve. "You mark my words. Gabriel is going to marry that girl."

> "Aw, Maeve," said Fergus, "she is a pretty lass. Any man in his right mind would take a good look."

Gabriel was an outgoing young man, a muddle of thoughts, tales and talking points. Shauna was shy, serene, soft-spoken, and certain. With her long curly brown hair pinned back from her divine face and soft green eyes, Shauna stood apart from the rest and was completely unaware of her sensuality.

It took months to convince her father that he would be an honourable husband.

"How much money does a writer make?" asked Shauna's father.

Gabriel shuffled uncomfortably. He didn't have an answer. Eventually, he disclosed what he was earning from his storytelling.

"Well, that's a lot more than I was expecting, lad," said Shauna's father, impressed. "If that's the case, I give you permission to marry his daughter right away!"

Gabriel and Shauna sat on the high cliffs that overlooked the sea. He took her hand and drew her closer. He got onto one knee as was required, and he proposed.

"I love you, Shauna. Will you be my wife?"

Shauna nodded, a smile filling her face as she flung her arms around his rugged neck.

"Is that a yes then?"

"Of course, it's a yes!" came the muffled reply.

They wed in the summer of 1843, married by the only priest in Drogheda whom the O'Donnell clan had not offended. Shauna wore a soft floral outfit, the communal wedding dress.

Moira O'Flaherty was in charge of it. Following the treasured item's use, the seamstress would inspect it stitch by stitch, repairing anything she deemed damaged. The gown would then be stored in a box until she needed to alter it for the next bride. The clothing's reappearance would be quite a spectacle thanks to a village custom. The valley's women would form a procession and carry the priceless garment to the bride's home, where it would be ceremoniously handed over.

Gabriel watched his wife walk into the church. This day, he had no words to describe what he was seeing. It was as if Shauna was walking toward him in a fluid pool of light. Her face was pure, innocent, and trusting. She took his breath away.

On their wedding night, Gabriel made love to his wife tenderly. For him, she was as delicate as the petals on a flower. In that moment, he decided he would sacrifice himself before he allowed anything to harm her.

20

THE BLIGHT

Fergus O'Donnell had heard it discussed in the pubs, and Gabriel had read it to him from the newspaper. He knew what he was seeing. The leaves of his potato crop were covered in huge black patches.

Fergus was dismayed. The British authorities had insisted that the blight was only prevalent in the West and South of Ireland. Fergus went home, hoping that he was wrong. He went onto his field and ripped a potato plant from the earth. The tubers had big ebony marks on them. They looked bruised. He cut the potato in half. The centre was mushy, and the flesh was black.

Hunched over, groaning, the ageing farmer was frantic. He ordered his sons and Gabriel to help unearth the crop in the hope that he would find some that were healthy.

"I want every tatie out of this earth today!"

They were exhausted, but they continued to toil. By sunset, they had taken out every potato in the field. All the tubers were stricken with blight.

The men stood in a group around their father. Fergus was typically a happy-go-lucky chap, but he was not stupid. That night was the most serious that Gabriel had ever seen him.

"It's reached us, he told his sons. We were daft to think that we were spared. We are a big family. Some of you have children of your own. We have two days to choose if we leave Ireland or if we stay here."

"This is all too sudden. This is our home, Pa! We have nothing. Where shall we go?" said one of the youngest, tearfully.

"I don't know, my boy. If we stay here, we will die, like they are dying in Munster."

"It will not get that bad here, Da. The government won't allow it."

"The queen has done nothing for Munster or Ulster. She'll not do anything for us," answered Fergus.

"America is the new world. They say there is land. We can farm. They will take us in."

"Da, this is happening too fast! We can't leave in two days. Where will the ticket money come from?"

"I have a nest egg," Fergus revealed.

*

Gabriel's first book had just been published by a brave London firm. The book had been mildly successful. He gave Fergus and Maeve everything that he earned. It was the least he could do since he owed Fergus and Maeve his life.

The arguments for and against continued well into the early hours of the morning. There was no resolution.

"Stop!" Fergus said.

Gabriel was surprised by Fergus's leadership. His usual nonchalance had left him, and now he was deathly serious.

"You have two days to decide what you are doing. Talk to your wives. Maeve and I have lived our lives. There is less risk to the decision for me. But you? You have children to raise and mouths to feed."

Two days later, it was unanimous. Three generations of O'Connells departed for Massachusetts. Choosing to stay with his new bride and her family, Gabriel travelled to Dublin with Fergus and Maeve. Saying goodbye to his adoptive parents broke his heart. His brothers, busy preparing to sail across the Atlantic, were his best friends. Everything he knew, and everyone he relied upon, was ripped away from him.

Feeling lost, he found a pub where he drank until he couldn't walk. For the first time in his newly married life, he arrived home drunk. Shauna took him into her arms, and he sobbed until he fell asleep from the alcohol and the grief.

A letter arrived a month later. Maeve and three of their grandchildren died on the ship. Bereft, Fergus returned to Ireland because he was too old to work, and his family began to splinter apart as soon as they arrived in New York. The land that promised them everything had rigorous selection criteria, which they didn't share until you arrived on their shore. Three sons had to head to Australia, a country that was looking for labourers. Two found their way to

Canada. The others did settle in America, where they found work in the coal mines of Pennsylvania. There they lived in dire poverty, far worse than they had in Ireland.

*

Gabriel and Shauna Craddick could afford food with the royalties he received from his book. It was not a lot of money, but it was enough to keep them away from the debtor's court.

During the day, Gabriel would look after his crop of peas, barley, and carrots, praying that there would be a harvest. It seemed that everything was a failure. The winter set in early, and the valley was a river of mud. All the tenants that were left were in fear of mudslides, the slow, silent killer that arrived without warning.

The whole character of the valley changed. People who had stood by each other for years were too afraid to share anything with their neighbours in case there was nothing tomorrow. People fought about food. Slowly but surely, there came a day when there was nothing to buy. Nobody could buy grain. The tax laws made it too expensive. There was no meal and flour for bread. Lots of produce was shipped back to England, with not a shred of it ending up for sale in Ireland.

Gabriel did the best he could with what he had. He was severely taxed by the British Exchequer, leaving him only half of what he earned, but he couldn't look at the money without guilt. He took a bit for him and Shauna and passed the rest along.

A black market for food developed, and thousands of people were shipped off to Australia for the sin of being hungry. Shauna Craddick never complained. She was a lot like Maeve. She could create a lot with very little.

Gabriel watched the British ships depart Drogheda, overloaded with food grown in Ireland. He was furious. All the Irishmen were furious but without means or energy to rebel. The Catholic church was overwhelmed. They couldn't maintain the demand for food and were being supported by the monies from parishes all over the Catholic world. The wealthiest Jewish bankers, Indians, Ottomans Sultan, Red Indians, Americans, French, Irish Americans, and many more gave money to feed the starving Irish. The Great Hunger saw every other country, creed, and colour at their best and the British government at their worst.

*

Gabriel watched a crowd of Turks offloading crates of food onto the shore of the Boyne River. He was desperate to feed his wife. The delicate girl that he had married was wasting away. A kind Turk threw him a bag of oatmeal. He took it and ran. If he could cook it in water and feed her, there was a chance that she would live.

Gabriel reached the cottage in the valley. His legs shook from running, and his heart raced. His starving body struggled to get oxygen from his lungs to his heart, and perspiration ran from him. Shauna was so emaciated that she was almost invisible in their bed. He reached her, and instinctively he knew that it was too late. Gabriel lay down next to her. He had failed on his promise to keep her safe. He stared into her eyes, but they were already glassy, somewhere between life and death. He lay next to her and took her in his arms. He didn't know if she could hear him, but he painted a picture of how much he loved her. When he was finished, he kissed her and closed her eyes. She had died while he was telling the story.

21

RAGE

Gabriel's fury ignited by reliving the terrible loss made him stand up and throw a chair across the cabin. And Finley rushed to stop him from throwing anything else not fixed down.

"I am so sorry for your pain. You must have been heartbroken."

"I wasn't heartbroken. I was murderous," Gabriel snapped.

"Do you know what it feels like to watch somebody die and have no means of helping them? Can you imagine if it was your husband and your child?"

It was a gut-wrenching question, and she had no answer for him.

"I promised her that I would look after her. I am as good as a murderer. I couldn't keep my promise. I vowed that there would be no other for the rest of my life. I promised that she was the only woman that I would ever love. Why did I live? I must have eaten more than she did, fended for myself better than I fended for her. My wife died because of me."

Finley tried to take his hand, but he pulled it away.

"That is why I can't send you to Scutari alone."

"I don't understand. Do you believe that you can redeem yourself by saving me?"

The question infuriated Gabriel even further, and he beat his fist on the desk. Finley blinked back tears.

"Do you think that you have the power to redeem me? Not even God will redeem me. Your family was comfortable. You had no conscience while you read the story in the newspaper every morning," he shouted at her.

"It's not true," she cried out, hurt by his accusation.

"Of course, it is true, while you were riding your pony, my wife was dying in my arms."

Finley felt as if he had knocked the wind out of her.

"I am taking you to Scutari because you don't know what it is to find someone you love dead."

Finley was horrified. How could he be that cruel? Closing her eyes, she relived the terrible night when her mother was mown down by the runaway horse.

"I don't know who you are anymore. You are a stranger to me, no more than a man that I met on a train," she growled, "who is as selfish as your father."

Gabriel seemed to buckle. He looked defeated, and he slumped onto a chair. His hair was a mess, his eyes were wild, and his clothing was shabby.

"I am nothing like my father was," Gabriel roared at her.

Finley ignored him. He was speaking to her back. She left the room and slammed the door behind her. Gabriel took a battered old hip flask from his case and took a good slug of brandy.

22

CONSTANTINOPLE

Finley stood on the deck of the steamship and looked up at the fairy-tale city. The Hagia Sophia, the splendorous mosque with four minarets, stood on the hill above the Bosporus. It had struggled for identity, battered between Christians and Muslims. The snow-covered minarets had witnessed centuries of war.

In the gloom of winter, it seemed to speak to Finley: 'I am as lonely as you are today. I also long for the warmth of the summer and peace for my people.'

The streets of the great cosmopolitan city were deserted, except for those who were forced to be outside. Ships were trapped in the harbour, surrounded by ice. Finley watched a pilot board the steamship. He would navigate them through the harbour and gently nudge them forward.

Finley had her knapsack at her feet. She was determined to make her way to Scutari without Gabriel by her side. She knew that she would be safe. She had been taught a lesson in Marseille, and her vigilance would not waver. Dressed as a man again, her hair was tucked under her hat. The great fur hood caught the snowflakes that gently drifted around her face.

Finley was the first person to disembark. Scutari was on the opposite side of the Bosporus, and she would need to take a ferry to reach it. She found a ferry master prepared to do the crossing, but it would be his last for the day. A storm was threatening. Finley could see the Scutari Hospital from where she stood. The imposing building, a former barracks, had been transformed into a hospital.

As she stepped ashore, she took her bearings. It was reaching late afternoon, and the temperature was dropping, and the wind was picking up speed. She was glad for her warm clothing. Reaching the hospital in the dark, she was escorted by driving snow rather than Gabriel.

*

A guard stopped her at the gate. She had removed her hat, and her hair was knotted in her neck. The guard eyed her suspiciously.

"What is your business, Miss?" he asked in a Geordie accent.

"I am looking for my father, Colonel Harrington, a Cavalry Officer."

"Have you received word from him?" asked the man.

"No, sir, but the high command in Malta told me that he is here."

"Thousands of men have come through here," said the guard. "I don't know where you would begin to search."

"Have you an escort?" he asked.

"No, sir, I am alone."

The guard shook his head. She was a brave young lady.

"Go there."

He pointed at an ornate arched door.

"Somebody will help you."

Finley knocked, but nobody answered. She let herself in. Standing in a great hallway, she saw a mass of corridors leading from it. A young doctor rushed past, then stopped abruptly, and approached her.

"Can I help you?" he asked. "Are you a new nurse here?"

"No. I am looking for someone."

"We have a register of the men who are here. There are more than a thousand at the moment. What is his name?"

"Colonel Harrington. Ernest. He was at the Battle of Balaclava."

The doctor felt sorry for her, and the possibility that he had survived the battle was slim.

"We have records of the soldiers who have arrived here, but it is not a complete list—"

The doctor composed his sentence before speaking.

"—there are those who arrived maimed and unrecognisable. Men are dying by the day, and we can't keep up."

"Can someone search the registers for me?"

"How far have you come?" he asked.

"From London."

"By Jove! Do you have a bed for the night?"

She shook her head.

"I will find somebody who can help you. Please wait here."

A nun appeared in the hallway. An older woman, she wore a simple habit and veil.

"My name is Sister Abigail," she told Finley. "The doctor said that you need help."

"Good evening, Sister. I am Finley Harrington. I am searching for my father, Colonel Ernest."

"This is an awkward hour to be searching for somebody. I think Captain Phillips is still on duty. He works in the clerical department. Come with me."

The nun showed Finley through a maze of corridors until they reached an elaborate office, finely decorated and polished.

A young officer greeted Finley. He saw her looking around the room.

"During peacetime, this is the office of the Ottoman Brigadier General," he explained.

"I am looking for my father."

"Where was he stationed?"

"He fought at Balaclava. Cavalry. Light brigade."

Captain Phillips knew that it was a hopeless search. More than half of the brigade was killed in the battle.

"The high command in Malta informed me that he was here."

"We have had an enormous number of casualties since that battle. Thousands of men. It will take time to find him, if he is here, that is. Perhaps you should return tomorrow?"

Finley felt tears in her eyes and fought to keep them in. It was pointless. They pushed over the brim and rolled down her cheeks.

"Now, now, Miss Harrington, don't cry," he said kindly.

Captain Phillips put his head out of the door and summoned Sister Abigail.

"I think Miss Harrington could do with a cup of tea, please? Make her comfortable, sister."

Finley followed the nun to a more practical side of the hospital.

"We have thirty-eight nurses, a contingent of nuns, and a large group of privates working here. We look after all the allied soldiers, French, Turks, Sardinians, and our own lads. Many of the local women assist with the nursing. Others do laundry and cleaning."

Finley heard what the nun was telling her, but she was distracted by the idea that her father could be lying some-where in the great barracks.

"Have you got accommodation in the town tonight?" asked Sister Abigail.

"No," Finley answered. "I didn't think to do that. I arrived on the ferry and came directly here."

"I believe that you will be allowed to stay, given your circumstances. We need to get permission from Miss Nightingale.

Finley nodded. She was too tired and disappointed to talk.

Sister Abigail knocked on a door and showed Finley into a large room. It was well lit, and there was a fire burning in the hearth. There was nothing ostentatious about the room. The only furniture worth remembering was a large ornate desk. Finley could see that the enormous room was used to capacity. Charts hung on the walls, and there was a large floor plan of the barracks.

A slight figure sat behind a large desk, concentrating on a document in front of her. She looked up when she heard them come into the room.

"Miss Harrington is on a mission to find her father," explained Sister Abigail.

The nun looked at Finley's curious outfit.

"How far have you come, my dear?"

"I have travelled from London," answered Finley, feeling honoured to be meeting such a famous woman in person.

"How may I help you?" Florence added with a smile.

"Captain Phillips is trying to find my father in the registers, and I need a place to sleep for the night."

"Of course, my dear. We will show you to a dormitory. The nurses will explain the rules to you. We have a severe cholera outbreak. There are strict protocols as to what to eat, drink and touch. You need to obey these rules throughout the hospital, including the dormitories."

"Yes, ma'am."

Finley reached her accommodation. There were a few people in it, but none of them was a nurse. The beds were narrow cots. A squat wood stove sat in the middle of the room. It was not hot, but comfortable. The day had taken its toll on Finley. Exhausted, she climbed on the cot fully clothed and flopped down on the hard mattress. Moments later, she was asleep.

The nuns fed Finley a breakfast of black tea and a grainy porridge. It was bland, but they assured her that it was nutritious and the only food in stock. The ice floes had played havoc with the army supply lines, and they were waiting for provisions.

"The situation is critical. Miss Nightingale has created a furore in England by publicising the plight of the hospital. But we have received a great amount of public support."

Ravenous, Finley ate everything that they gave her, appreciating every mouthful. Finley went to see Captain Phillips after breakfast.

"I have searched every register since the Battle of Balaclava, but I can't find your father's name anywhere."

"Are there any other men here that survived the battle?"

"I know of one man, but he is extremely ill with cholera. We daren't go near those wards. Only the nurses are allowed there. It is terrible. Up to four hundred men die there a day."

The figure was too large for Finley to comprehend.

"We bury them around the clock. More men are dying from cholera than from wounds."

"Why do they become so ill?"

"The squalor here means drinking mostly dirty water that contains, well—" he stammered. "You know what."

Finley thought she knew what he meant.

"Miss Nightingale is insisting that the sewer system be rebuilt."

"That must be very challenging for her, being a woman? Giving men orders?"

"She is an angel. We have seen an enormous difference since she arrived, but people are still dying in their hundreds each day."

"What is the name of the man who fought at Balaclava?" She changed the subject.

"Sergeant Dennis Brown hails from the Midlands somewhere."

"Is he one of those with cholera?"

"Luckily not. He is an amputee."

Finley raised her eyebrows.

"As you know, Miss Harrington, we can't identify every man, but according to our records, he has never come here."

As always, Finley had difficulty accepting defeat. She had travelled to Scutari for a purpose, to find her father, and she wouldn't leave without him.

*

Gabriel Craddick looked for his companion, but he couldn't find her, and he was frantic. He knew that she was fractious, but he hadn't anticipated that she would leave without him.

"Are you looking for Miss Harrington?" asked the captain.

"Yes. Have you seen her?"

"Mr Craddick, you may have missed the opportunity of a lifetime. She was the first person to disembark the ship. I watched her walk towards the ferry."

"Was she with anyone?"

"No. She went alone."

Gabriel raced down the wharf towards the ferry. He reached the jetty where the boat was moored.

"Good evening," he shouted. "Do you speak English?"

"What do you want?" a gruff Turkish voice replied.

"I need to get to Scutari as fast as I can."

The man looked him up and down before shouting:

"Look around you. Look at the weather. Can you see the ice on the water? The ferry is closed."

"Who can take me. I will pay?"

"Everybody can pay. But nobody has enough money to replace my boat if it sinks."

"Do you know anyone who will help me?"

"No, now get off my jetty and stop asking stupid questions. Bloody Englishman."

"Irish, not English. And don't you forget it."

Gabriel didn't know whom to be more furious with, Finley or himself. After some introspection, he accepted that two people had called him stupid in one day, and so there had to be some truth in it.

He looked for a small hotel in the ancient city and found one in a crooked little side street. So anxious to find Finley, he had not realised how cold it was. Mist lay over the water. The visibility was poor. A dull lamp hung at the door of the hotel and cast a gloomy glow on the snow. The windows were dirty, and it looked cold inside. It reminded him of the lodgings in Malta.

This time, the room had more furniture and a small coal stove, making it much more welcoming than the reception. Gabriel looked out of the window. There were rows of houses, and he could see the warm light peeping through the windows. It reminded him of the valley in Ireland. He imagined the families tucked up warm inside.

He felt lonely and wanted to go home. He pined for his family. He longed for the warmth and comfort of the cottage. He wanted to sit at the fire again and hear Fergus squabble with Maeve. Poor old Maeve. How he missed her. As his heart reacted with emotion, his mind replied with logic.

It finally resonated with him that the valley was empty. That life was gone, smashed apart like a bottle thrown against a wall, never to reappear again. The cottages were gone. The O'Donnells' were scattered around the world. Shauna would never return, even if he spent his whole life wishing that she would.

He examined his promise to Shauna that she would be the only woman he would ever love. He grasped that Shauna's body had died, and her soul had been spirited into a blissful energy where she was whole again. But why would she want him to be broken?

It was the most significant choice that Gabriel would make in years. He chose to retain the memory of Shauna but set his conscience free of the guilt of failing her. Millions of Irish had died. He would also have died if it weren't for the ships that brought food to Drogheda. He had been granted a reprieve, a second chance. The only way to show his gratitude was to live a full life.

23

SCUTARI

Finley thanked Captain Phillips for his help and bade him farewell. The captain took it for granted that the unexpected visitor knew the directions to the front door and didn't need an escort.

After walking down the long corridors, she reached an intersection. The exit was to the right and the large wards to the left. She understood the gravity of what she was about to do and decided to accept the risks.

Turning left, Finley opened the door slowly and boldly stepped into another corridor. Still dressed in men's clothes, she hoped that it would help conceal her as she began to search for Dennis Brown.

She entered a long ward with high arched windows, lined with so many beds that she couldn't count them from where she stood. She deduced it was a cholera ward from the terrible odour that emanated from it. Quickly backtracking, she closed the great doors softly behind her.

She opened another door and spotted some patients walking about, so she slipped in. It was another long room. She estimated there were a hundred beds. At the far end was another door.

Although Finley felt intimidated, she saw a soldier sitting on his bed and asked for help. Her clothing didn't fool the fellow.

"By gods, lads! Here we have an angel doing her rounds," he laughed cheerfully.

Finley smiled.

"You are very happy for a sick man," she laughed.

"If you saw where we came from, this is paradise, lass."

"I am looking for someone. A chap called Dennis Brown."

"Oh miss, there are probably thirty Dennis Browns in this rabble," he sighed.

"He is an amputee," Finley added, hoping it would help.

He shook his head:

"Nah."

"He is a cavalry officer. In the Light Brigade at Balaclava."

The man's face lit up.

"That Dennis Brown. Well, now I can help you, lass," he said, patting her hand. "They have all those chaps in the same ward. Continue down the corridor, and right at the bottom, you'll find them."

"Thank you, sir. Thank you so much."

She squeezed his hand and beamed a glorious smile.

"It's a pleasure, me darling. You have made me day."

Finley followed his instructions and found the door she was looking for. A few nurses passed her, but they ignored her. She walked down the centre of the ward, it was clean, and once again, there was a stove in the middle of the room. The men were covered in scratchy grey blankets. As she moved along from bed to bed, she studied each man's face hoping to find her father. All of them were severely wounded at Balaclava, which was weeks ago but had still not recuperated. Some slept, others moaned, clutching at bandaged limbs or bloated bellies. There was a bit of laughter here and there. She saw two men in better fettle playing chess. A few others sat on their beds, talking to each other.

"Good morning," she said with a smile. "Please, can you help me?"

The man saw through her disguise immediately.

"Ooh, anything for a looker like you, Miss," he said, raising his eyebrows mischievously.

"I am looking for Sergeant Dennis Brown."

"Oi, Dennis. A pretty girl is waiting to see you," the man shouted across the ward.

Fearful of being discovered by a jobsworth official, Finley laughed nervously, then bowed her head.

"Who is it?" another Geordie voice asked.

" Finley Harrington," she called back.

The ward came to a standstill. All those who Finley had thought were asleep began to slowly sit up in their beds. It was like the dead were rising. A man on crutches came from the far side of the room, whom she assumed was Dennis Brown. He seemed pleasant enough.

"How are you, er, Dennis?"

"Aye, Dennis. That's me. Truthfully? I am glad I am not in Balaclava," he told her. "It is a memory that I will never erase. The battle was devastating, but it was worse afterwards."

Finley looked into the man's eyes. His sunny disposition had faded to grey, and it was replaced with a blank stare.

"They lay the dead out in rows. I have never seen so many dead men. It took weeks to bury them. Our friends, men we had known all our lives, rotted away before our eyes. The smell, I will never forget the smell. It will sit in my nostrils for the rest of my life. The wounded were trapped in the valley. They had no way to move us. The horses that were shot we ate. It became a valley of hell. How we can claim we won anything, I don't know."

"And your leg?" asked Finley.

"Well, I got a piece of shrapnel in it, here, just above the knee."

He showed Finley, who flinched at the sight of the wound.

"The field doctors dug it out of me. They didn't know what to do with us. Most of the doctors were young lads. They weren't ready for what they saw."

Finley could feel his despair, but she could only listen.

"We waited weeks before they put us on a boat and brought us here. We were freezing, starving. This leg had turned black, and I started a fever."

Dennis Brown's face went snow white.

"They cut my lower limb off with a saw, like the saw you would find in yer granddaddy's shed. They gave me a bottle of whiskey and told me to drink the lot. Then, they gave me opium. It was bearable while they cut through the flesh, but I felt everything when they reached the bone. The pain is stamped into me brain, lass. I don't know how to make it go away."

Finley couldn't identify what she was feeling. It was a combination of shock, sorrow, and humility.

"I just want to go home, lass. Me and the lads—" he made a sweeping movement with his arm, "— we just want to go home."

It seemed that all the bravado and humour were sucked out of the room, and there was a void of despair. Finley felt guilty. She had not come to upset them, but unwittingly, she had.

"You have come a long way in search of your Da."

"Yes, sir."

"He stood in the front line of the battle, the thin red line they call it now," said Dennis Brown, shaking his head. "What a bloody mess that was."

"Do you know if he is alive?"

"He was wounded. We all were wounded or dead. When it was over, and there was almost nobody left to kill. People arrived to help us. Strangers. I saw him being pulled off the battlefield."

"Did the Russian army capture him?"

"No, they were long gone. I reckon they were locals. Not the military, judging by what they were wearing."

"Where should I look, sir? I am not going home without him."

"There is a small settlement close to Balaclava. It is called Ternivka. There is an orthodox church there. Maybe one of the clerics took him in. Thank God if they did, Miss Harrington—because he may still be alive."

Back in Constantinople, Gabriel was at his wits' end.

24

CHRISTMAS AT SEA

Finley made her way to the ferry. Her day had been fruitful but disturbing. She couldn't erase Dennis Brown's words from her mind. Like all women, she struggled to find a reason that justified slaughtering humans to win a piece of land, or because you didn't like them, or they had more ships than you did.

She reached the wharf and was pleased to see the ferry was in operation. She was the only person on board, but the man took her across anyway. She saw a lone figure on the wharf waiting for the ferry. It was Gabriel.

He walked past her and stood at the mooring.

> "You said you weren't working, you rotter," he yelled at the Turk.

> "She is prettier than you, Englishman," he shouted.

> "Irishman, you swine."

*

They didn't greet each other.

> "What happened at the hospital?" he demanded.

"I met a man who told me that father may be in Ternivka."

"Where on God's green earth is that?"

"A small settlement close to Balaclava."

"That's almost five hundred miles away."

"I said I will find him, and the Black Sea, cold or war, won't stop me."

Gabriel didn't argue. He had learnt his lesson. He knew she would do it with or without him.

He saw a steamship some distance away and ran toward it, almost losing his footing on the ice. They were loading cargo even though they were snowed in.

"I need to go to Balaclava," he told the first mate.

"God help you," said the officer.

"Never mind that. Who can get me there?"

"There are two ships in open water, both heading in that direction."

"How do I reach them?"

"Row. One is laying a sub-marine communication cable, the other is a royal naval vessel fetching the wounded."

"Which is the best choice?"

"The transporter—it will be empty."

They found a man who was prepared to take them to the ship.

"State your business," shouted the officer on deck.

"I need to reach Balaclava," Gabriel answered.

"We don't take passengers," returned the man.

"The lady has come all the way from London to find her father."

"What is his name?"

"Colonel Ernest Harrington."

"By crikey! You're in luck. I have heard of him." said the crewman. "Come aboard."

The officer admired Finley. She was a lovely young woman. Her dress code was unorthodox but a wise choice.

"We have a cabin available for the lady, and you can bunk with the men."

Gabriel paid the oarsman double the amount that he had asked for. They climbed up the ladder and onto the deck. Finley did it without effort. It was pitch dark and below freezing.

"We will serve you dinner, Miss. This is a modern steamer. There is a small stove in your cabin to keep you warm. The rest of the ship is empty. We need as much space as we can find to transport the wounded. Poor blighters have been stranded for months."

"What time do we sail?" asked Gabriel.

"First light."

Finley went to her cabin and soaked up the gentle heat from the stove. Next, she washed, ate the basic meal she was provided and went to sleep. In the early hours of the morning, there was a knock on the door. Gabriel called her name. She was not even tempted to open the door and instead turned over and went back to sleep.

Finley rested for two days. An officer gave her a book to read, and she relished in the peace of her own company.

On the third day, Finley went on deck, thin layers of ice drifted on the sea. Gabriel had spent a significant amount of time on deck, hoping to see Finley, and today he was lucky. 'I am sorry,' were his first words.

Finley was not afraid of confrontation, and she was certainly not afraid of Gabriel.

"I am not a part of your history," she told him. "I am not responsible for what you suffered, and I am not ashamed of where fate put me. My father has fought for years, keeping the enemy off British soil, and that includes Ireland. He has been prepared to give his life to protect it."

Gabriel looked at the floor and turned his back on her.

"You can turn your back on me, but it will not change the truth. Your ghosts have turned to demons. I won't wait for you. I won't walk in the shadow of another woman. I won't wait for some

day in the distant future when you decide that
you can live with yourself."

Gabriel had underestimated her. She was young but not
stupid.

"What can I do to prove that I love you?" he
asked abruptly.

Finley was taken aback by the admission. No man had ever
said that to her before.

"I am here. I have come to help you," he begged.
"Isn't that enough for you?"

"I can help myself. And no, it is not enough for
me."

Gabriel reached out to touch her, but she pushed his hand
away again. *How dare he assume that I would fall into his
arms.*

She watched him walk away. For a brief moment, she re-
gretted that she had been so bristly, but it was fleeting.
Finley wanted to marry for love—real love—not a love
with dark shadows. Every time that he was sullen and
brooding, she didn't want to be in fear that he was mourn-
ing Shauna. Repeatedly, she told herself there were many
men in the world, yet the words always rang hollow. When
her head listened to her heart, it told her the only man she
wanted was Gabriel Craddick.

*

There was a knock on her door. It wasn't Gabriel, but a
cabin boy with a message for her.

"The captain requests your company in the dining room at seven o'clock this evening."

It was an unusual invitation and unorthodox, given that she would be the only woman, but she accepted.

"Thank you for joining us, Miss Harrington."

She smiled as she walked towards the skipper.

"Thank you for considering me."

"Our cook has prepared a little something for us, and the men wish to have a little celebration before they reach Balaclava. There will be no time to celebrate Christmas with all the work to be done, so they have decided that this is as good a time as any to have a bit of cheer."

The captain led her into the dining table, and as he pulled back her chair, she was aware of a familiar smell—mince pies, the most comforting aroma in the world. It was rich and sweet and reminded her of home. The table was dressed in the finest linen and covered with Christmas fayre. Soon roasted goose, potatoes, pork pies, apples, plums, and Christmas pudding appeared. She could see a bowl of punch, bottles of wine and decanters of whiskey. Best of all was her favourite, eggnog with a sprinkle of delicious nutmeg on top.

Gabriel leant against the opposite wall and saw the delight in her eyes. They were warm and sparkled in the lamplight. She had a comfortable grace and greeted all the men around her. They were intrigued by the beautiful lady in men's clothing. The cook came out of the galley and bowed to great applause. There was a distinct camaraderie between the men. It reminded her of her brothers.

Gabriel observed the group. They were on a ship in the middle of an icy sea, going to a country ravaged by war, but could still celebrate the wonder of Christmas. Finley was correct. For ten years, he had been self-indulgent. He had lost precious time wallowing in self-pity. He had loved Shauna, but he couldn't remember her face with the same clarity anymore. These days, when he closed his eyes, he saw a new face.

A man began to sing 'Silent Night', and the others joined him. The moment was surreal. The squally weather made the creaking steamer pitch, but the men were still in fine voice.

Finley watched Gabriel leave. The Irishman went onto the deck and stood in the silence. Gripping the handrail, with his hair blown away from his face, he could hear the Christmas carol resonating through the ship and spill out into the black night. He had hurt the woman he loved. He had to win her back. How would he convince her that the time for them had arrived sooner than he had led her to believe? He pondered the situation until he had an inkling of a plan.

Finley's cabin door rattled on its hinges as he thumped his palm against it. There was no response.

"If you don't open this door, I will break it down."

A bleary-eyed Finley, dressed for bed in Fatima's kaftan, unlocked the door. The burly Irishman barged his way past. Before she could object, he spoke.

"I love you, Finley. I don't want to waste another moment of my life in the past. I don't want to live my life haunted by things I can't change."

She looked at him sceptically then turned her back.

"Finley, don't do this. Don't walk away from me."

His voice sounded anguished. He was struggling to keep his composure.

"Don't lose your temper with me, Gabriel. It is a very ugly trait. You've done nothing but snap at me recently."

Gabriel put his head back and ran his hands through his hair, frustrated.

"You were happy to use me to secure your passage from Marseille, weren't you, Finley? Now you're almost at your destination, you couldn't care less about me! I've served my purpose, I suppose. Well? What do you have to say for yourself?"

She was in love with him and wanted him more than he would ever know, but she didn't have an answer for him. Gabriel stormed out of the room and slammed the door. Moments later, he was back with his book in his hand.

"Get dressed," he commanded.

He began throwing clothes at her.

"Now! I'll be back."

In a furious temper, she got dressed. On his return, he gave her no time to protest, grabbed her hand and dragged her up onto the deck. He pulled her toward the railing.

"Look at me," he shouted, "I love you. If this does not convince you, nothing will."

She watched him open the book. He began to pull out the pages. Then he tore the pages to shreds. Soon, his carefully penned words were destroyed. He threw the tattered cover overboard. The last of torn fragments twirled in the wind, then descended into the darkness, settling on the waves, the words were lost forever. All the while, the steamer plunged forward, leaving Gabriel's past behind him.

25

SHADOWY FIGURES

Finley's brothers stood looking at the colossal reels taming the great cables that would be laid across the Black Sea. Running run along the seabed and into the Mediterranean, the cables would join the Middle East to the West. Born out of necessity, the allied governments thought this trailblazing engineering project would save lives.

The four Harrington brothers left London the moment they received her letter from Marseille. Not only were they concerned about their father, but they were also terrified for their sister. They understood that she was headstrong and determined, but this time 'she had bitten off more than she could chew.'

The vessel they were on was delayed in Malta, and they were forced to spend three days in a shabby little hotel. The place had been cold, threadbare, and spartan. The British high command in Malta had heard that the Harringtons were in Valletta. A young private had dropped off a message. Lester told his siblings:

You are invited to meet with the brigadier regarding Colonel Ernest Harrington.

RSVP

They arrived at a beautiful building and were escorted into the office of Brigadier Grayling. The man was professional, distinguished and displayed sincere empathy.

"We have found your father," he told them. "He is in a small village close to Balaklava, Ternivka. It is a small settlement. The people are kind."

"Is he alive?"

"When we received the intelligence, he was, yes. But we haven't had any more news."

The men looked sombre. Lester spoke for them.

"Brigadier, our sister, Finley Harrington, may have passed through here?"

"Now you mention it, yes she did. Some days ago. She gave General Logan a good beating on the wharf," laughed the brigadier.

"Oh! Sorry about that."

"Not to worry, between you and me, Logan probably deserved it. When General Logan left here a few days ago, he had two black eyes."

Lester wondered if Grayling knew about the photograph in The Times. It seemed there was no escape from the scandal.

"Do you know where she was going to?"

"Yes. Scutari."

"But you say that my father is in Ternivka?" Lester quizzed.

"You may be interested to know that she was not alone. She had a guide with her, a rather unusual fellow. He was a bit of a hooligan, an Irishman. We later learnt that his name was Gabriel Craddick. We have a troopship heading to evacuate a lot of our men. We suspect the two of them charmed their way onto that vessel. We shall be having words with the captain on his return."

*

Eleanor Harrington was elated. It was the best Christmas gift she could have hoped for. She had received word from General Logan that he had been given a brief assignment in The Crimea, and then he would return to England. Before his departure, he had sworn his undying love and promised that he would put a roof over her head and that she would never be alone. He went on to tell her it was a lovely warm little place, and they would be content.

Eleanor's mind raced. She imagined Luxembourg and Monaco. She could imagine the soirees with the elite, the magnificent gala dinners, and the pleasure of a regal society. Oh, how she longed to entertain in those circles.

Logan decided that only when she got onto the ship would he tell her that they were departing for a beautiful remote island in the Indian Ocean, Madagascar.

*

The brothers returned to their hotel, relieved that they had word of their sister but were concerned that she was travelling with a man deemed a hooligan.

They would stay on the next ship until it reached Balaclava.

26

TERNIVKA

Finley's ship docked at Balaclava. Low black clouds hung just above their heads. There were no proper moorings because the small inlet was littered with crippled and sunken naval vessels. Tall masts reached out above the water, and flotsam was washed up on the beaches. What was once a scenic bay was now a ship's graveyard.

Pockets of men were strewn between the wreckage. They were wrapped in every piece of clothing that they could find, even the clothes of the naked, emaciated corpses they shared their tents with. The beleaguered men's eyes lit up when they saw the last hope of rescue puffing towards them.

Finley could see animal entrails and human waste drifting in on the incoming tide. The men had hoped that the current would carry it away. Instead, it wound around the wreckage and stewed until it poisoned the sea and the surrounding water sources. The wind was blowing off the land, bringing the stench of disease and decay with it.

Mr Russell, The Times' correspondent, had described it correctly. It was hell on earth. As oarsman rowed them ashore, some of the sailors wretched over the side of the little wooden boat. Finley stared at the horror around her, but it only galvanised her resolve. *'Somewhere on this piece of earth that God has deserted lies my father. I will find him, even if I die doing it.'* The boat hit the shore with a sliding crunch.

"Careful with your footing, lads." said the oarsman. "The snow is a foot deep. And the locals say that there is more coming. We need to get these fellas out sharpish."

Flimsy tents dotted the surrounding hills. They had housed the wounded for weeks.

"Don't touch anyone or anything," Gabriel instructed her. "These men have cholera and typhus. We are not helping them by getting ill."

He helped her out of the boat, and they struggled up the hillside. The snow was fresh, and their legs sank into it until their feet reached frozen unpredictable earth below. They saw a pathway trampled through the thick blanket of white and followed it.

On reaching a khaki field tent plastered with ice, Gabriel opened the flap and looked in. His jaw fell. There were around seventy men in there, huddled together for warmth.

"How do we reach Ternivka?" Gabriel shouted into the tent.

Nobody answered. Nobody cared. Stepping back out into the frozen landscape, Gabriel saw two houses which served as barracks and headed towards them. He was relieved that Finley was fit and athletic. Dragging a prissy girl around would have been exhausting.

An officer sat at a desk greeted them. Surprised to see a woman, he stumbled to his feet.

"We are heading to Ternivka," Gabriel told him, "How far is it from here?"

"Not far. A few hills away. There is a road," replied the officer, retaking his seat.

"Do you have horses available?"

"As men abandoned by the government, left to rot in this hellhole, we eat horses—we don't ride them."

Gabriel took that to mean no.

"Accommodation?" he asked.

"Yes, we have plenty. Choose any of the tents you see around the hills. I advise you to choose one without deadly disease," replied the surly fellow.

Gabriel was becoming annoyed with the man's sarcasm.

"Can you give us more information than that?"

"No, sir," replied the officer, distracted by a top-secret document lying on his desk.

Gabriel beat his fist on the table in frustration, and the official jumped in fright. Finley knew the rules of war. She gave Gabriel a look that meant 'let me handle this', then intervened.

"I am searching for my father. A colonel," she said firmly.

"Name?"

Gabriel was pleased to see the man had the decency to look at her.

"Ernest Harrington."

"Why did you not say that to start with?" he chastised the pair.

"Your father is being cared for by a woman four miles North of Ternivka."

"How can you be sure? The army said that they didn't know where he was?" Finley quizzed.

"A young Armenian man saved him. Dragged him all that way. Heaven knows why. Our scouts told us that his old crone of a mother was nursing your father in the hills."

"How long have you known?"

"Since the battle."

"Why did you not communicate this to us?" Finley demanded.

"We are very busy, Miss Harrington. Evacuating the men has been our priority here, not sending messages to loved ones."

Finley tried to dive over the desk and grab the indifferent man by his lapels, but Gabriel stopped her just in time.

"She was about to assault me!" shrieked the man.

"It's a good job I stopped her," snapped Gabriel. "I was about to sucker punch you myself."

*

"You must stop attacking British Officers, Finley.
You will get us thrown in the stocks."

Finley began to laugh. It was the funniest moment that they
had shared for a long time.

"I wanted to thump him but remembered how
much my hand hurt last time."

The moment was tender. Gabriel tried to reach for her hand
and pull her closer, but she gave him the slip. Instead, they
climbed the snow-laden hill six feet apart.

*

It was early afternoon, but it was becoming dark, exacerbated by the clouds. Her knapsack was heavy, but Finley
was determined to carry her own load. Gabriel coaxed, encouraged, and made her laugh. He tried to cheer her up, but
it was clear the burden of worry about her father was dragging the smile from her face.

The walk to Ternivka took longer than they anticipated.
Fighting blizzard conditions across land covered with
treacherous ice, it was slow going. At the brow of the hill,
they saw another area dotted with tattered, abandoned
tents. Finley blinked back tears as she realised, she was
overlooking the battlefield where her father was last seen.

"We need a place to settle for the night, Finley.
It's almost dark."

"I was told there is a hospital in that nearby
church—"

"—but it will be full of men riddled with disease. You will have to trust me," said Gabriel. "Let's push on until we see some trees or caves to shelter by."

Half a mile later, they saw a small patch of forest. There was no colour in the blackened landscape.

"The Russians burnt down everything when they retreated," said Finley.

"Even better," Gabriel cheered, his optimism puzzling the girl.

Gabriel slogged through the snow, inspecting the largest tree trunks still standing.

"Here!" he yelled.

Finley wiped the hair from across her eyes and trudged across to him.

"This tree has been burnt hollow, Fin. We will stay in it for the night."

"We will never fit into that little annexe. It's too small," she complained.

"We have no choice. And you will be happy that it's small. It will make it much easier to keep each other warm."

Finley looked dismayed. The plan seemed futile. Darkness was upon them, and the temperature had plummeted.

"I think we should push on to the church."

"And break our necks falling down a ravine? I
don't think so. If hiding in tree trunks can work
for wolves out here, it will work for us."

Finley squeezed herself into the small space, the size of a
single wardrobe. Eleanor's furry hood caught on a piece of
bark as she bent double to get in. Once inside, she pulled
her knees up, and they almost reached her nose. Gabriel
wrestled his way in and grabbed her knapsack, then
plugged the entrance.

"Our bags will be a good barrier against the cold.
Thank God the wind is finally dying down. Do you
have food in that bag?"

"A few scraps of cheese, bread, some meat, mince
pies. All rock hard."

"Sounds delicious," he chuckled before becoming
more serious. "We need food in our stomachs."

Gabriel dug in his bag and pulled out a candle, matches, and
a pair of enamel mugs. He shoved his arm through the hole
and scooped up two cupsful of snow.

A rough scratching sound was followed by the golden
crackling of a lit match. Gabriel pushed the flame against
the candlewick as soon a welcoming, warm glow filled the
space. He took the food and pushed it down the neck of his
coat. Finley looked mildly disgusted.

"We'll break our teeth on this otherwise," he
joked.

Next, he carefully swirled the icy water in the mug. A sooty
black mark formed on the base as the drink warmed up.
When it was just past tepid, he passed the cup to her. In that

bleak moment, it was the best drink that Finley had ever tasted, even though it was flavourless.

They ate the slightly thawed food and sipped more hot water. It was a dinner they would remember for the rest of their lives.

"Why on earth did you think of bringing candles?" Finley laughed at him. "I thought you only had your pens in that case of yours? Now your book has sunk to the bottom of the sea?"

"One candle in a small space can keep you from freezing to death," he said sombrely.

The inside of the trunk of damp but not wet, and they shuffled around until they were comfortable but entwined like a Chinese puzzle. Once air temperature was bearable, he blew out the candle, and darkness returned.

"You are the bravest woman I know, Miss Harrington."

"I—would never have been able to make this journey by myself," she confessed.

"Nobody can journey by themselves," he said gently. "We all need someone beside us."

Silence returned. They were both too exhausted for idle chat.

"What day is it?" asked Finley, who had lost track of time.

"Christmas eve," laughed Gabriel.

He fumbled in the gloom, took her hand, and squeezed it.

"This is an unusual way to celebrate Christmas," Finley chuckled.

"I told you that I celebrate Christmas differently."

Finley laughed and nudged into him with her shoulder.

"You!"

She snuggled her head against his.

"Will you?"

"Will I what?"

"Tell me one of your stories, Gabriel?"

"Tonight is not a night for stories, Fin. Tonight I need to tell you the truth."

Finley's eyes widened. After hearing about his decade of yearning for his wife, she had hoped there were no more hidden depths to the man, no more unpalatable things to confess. He felt her flinch.

"Don't be afraid. This is not a story or a fantasy. Merely what I know to be true in my heart."

"—And," croaked a little voice.

"Next Christmas, you will be sitting with me in front of a blazing fire. We'll be at my home in Geneva. You will no longer be Finley Harrington. You will be my wife, the delightful Mrs Craddick."

He paused. Finley said nothing.

"The last weeks are the best I have had for years, and you are the bravest and strongest woman that I have ever met, and I need someone brave to tolerate me," he admitted.

"Is that so? I can't say I'd noticed you could be difficult?" she teased.

He turned his head to hers and lifted her chin. The night was freezing, but the kiss was like a fire between them. Despite her youth and inexperience, that second kiss told her Gabriel Craddick loved her with all his heart and that he was a good man.

"Come on. Put this Irish fellow out of his misery. Will you marry me, Fin?" he asked tenderly.

"Of course, I will," she replied before initiating a kiss of her own.

When they fell apart, if had it been light, her fiancée would have seen joyful tears in her eyes and a broad smile.

Peace descended upon their nest. Gabriel shuffled the bags that were protecting them and peeked out into the night.

"Look Fin, look," he told her.

She looked through the gap and smiled.

Miraculously, there was a small break in the clouds, and the brightest star that she had ever seen was twinkling, as if just for them. The clouds snapped shut, and the star disappeared as fast as it had arrived. Still, it was a sign from the heavens that there was hope.

27

THE PERFECT GIFT

They waited until the sun was up and providing light before they moved from the shelter. It didn't add much warmth, but at least they could see where they were going. Before heading off, Gabriel put his arms around her, and they kissed. He kissed her mouth, then her eyes, smothering her whole face in kisses. He put his head back and laughed in delight.

"Merry Christmas, Fin."

He kissed her again.

"Have you forgotten I need to find my father?" she said, making haste towards the hills in the distance. "Come on. The kissing can wait."

It was perishingly cold, regardless of morning, noon, or night, sun, or clouds. Their hands grew stiff. Clutching the cups of water without gloves on hurt their hands. As soon as the drink was quaffed, they had to keep moving else risk exposure. Finley pulled out a meagre ration of food from time to time, and they ate as they walked.

Yesterday's blizzard meant there was a new layer of snow, and the road was more treacherous than before. It glistened in the sunlight. For once, they were no side-by-side. Gabriel led, and Finley followed in his footsteps.

In the distance, a plume of smoke curled and climbed into the air, a sliver of grey in a sea of white. Far behind them, Gabriel spotted some shadowy figures following them.

"Come on. Let's keep up the pace," he insisted, not sure if they were pursued by friend or foe.

Reaching the summit of a hill, they saw some little buildings below them in a valley. Gabriel thought of Ireland for a moment but then pushed the memory to the back of his mind. He would not look back. He would never look back again.

In the centre of the simple dwellings stood a tiny church, barely enough for a congregation of fifty souls. Smaller plumes of smoke arose from the crooked chimneys.

"Quickly. That must be it. The place I was told about at Scutari."

Finley pressed on through the snow with renewed vigour, despite toppling over every few steps. When they reached the great doors, they were hesitant to enter. They hid to one side of the entrance.

"What do we do now?" she whispered breathlessly.

The decision was taken out of their hands. The wooden double doors opened. A comforting wave of warm air wafted out as parishioners began to peel out into the country lane, all holding torches aloft, lit like giant matches.

In a state of constant vigilance, the villagers soon spotted the strangers. There had been so many over the years. They didn't know who to trust. All those processing ignored the couple, except for a young man with bright eyes and a wide grin. He greeted them in an unrecognisable language. He realised his attempt at communicating was futile and almost gave up. Then he tried again in French. As the man talked, the faint flame on his torch gave out. Gabriel, Finley, and man gesticulated to each other and tried to get along in broken French, both parties only understanding a few words.

"Monsieur Harrington. Il est mon père. Il est—uh—inju—blessé. Err, I—je pense—um—he is here—ici?" said Finley, with terrible pronunciation.

"'Arrington? Oui, Oui!"

He pointed at a cottage in the distance. The man smiled broadly and nodded.

"*Davit*," he said, proudly patting his chest.

"Merci, Davit," she said, putting a hand on her heart. "Je suis Finley, et c'est Gabriel."

She pointed to the Irishman, hoping that her translation was correct. Davit smiled, and she saw the sincerity in his eyes.

The local fellow grabbed her by the hand and led her into the tiny orthodox church. It was surprisingly warm, given the harshness of the weather outside. Everything inside was beautiful. The nave was lined with wooden icons, all exquisitely gilded. It was the pride of the humble community.

Davit pointed at the smouldering baton and then a large candle.

"Lueur Christ loger," Davit said cryptically.

He mimed reigniting the torch and then processing, and Gabriel understood immediately.

"He must mean that they take the light of Christ from the church to their house."

Finley was touched by the tradition and smiled at Davit. The man passed the torch to Finley, who offered it to the candle and watched the tip snap and crackle into flame. They processed out of the church. Davit beckoned Finley, and Gabriel followed him.

Outside, Davit was determined to introduce them to the priest, and they waited in line to receive the man's blessings and introduce themselves. Gabriel looked up towards the hilltop. The dark figures that had been following them all morning were closing in on the village. The sight convinced him it was he and Finley who were their target. Concerned, Gabriel wondered what to do. He was worried General Logan might have sent out a party to thwart their plans. He decided it was best to stay with the locals than make a run for it. 'Safety in numbers.' The snow began to fall heavily again.

By now, the men were close. They were heavily covered against the cold. It looked like they were making their way toward the small church in search of shelter.

As they drew closer, Finley was convinced she heard a familiar voice. She turned sharply to see a man running towards her, struggling in the snow. Gabriel positioned himself between the two of them.

An incredulous Finley saw her beloved brother Clive running towards her.

"Finley!" yelled a voice.

"Clive? It can't be!"

The two siblings staggered towards each other as the other figures trudged over.

"Well, you took your time," she teased. "It's my brothers, Gabriel! They have finally come to help."

"Fin, you've led us on one hell of a journey," shouted Lester.

Gabriel sympathised with a hearty belly laugh. He knew that he and the Harrington men would be good friends.

"Merry Christmas, they shouted to each other."

The meeting was surreal. Nobody would have imagined how sweet the reunion would be.

"Excusez-moi! Monsieur 'Arrington? Oui?" beckoned Davit.

They formed a line behind the man as he walked towards a small cottage high above them.

"Pourquoi aidez-vous?" asked Clive.

Davit rubbed his tummy and smiled. They took that to mean Ernest Harrington had fed him some of his army rations when he was rescued from the battlefield.

They climbed the icy path. Davit carried the flickering torch, and they followed it like the star of Bethlehem. As they got closer, they understood how humble the abode was. The war had taken its toll on everything, people, houses, animals, forests. There was no exemption.

"Have you got food in those knapsacks?" Finley asked Lester.

"Of course," he replied, patting the plump bag on his back.

"We will feed these people today."

Lester smiled at his sister, and Gabriel took her hand once more.

*

Davit opened the door into the humble cottage. The interior was one large room with a stone floor. There was a table made of rough wood in the middle of the room with one unlit candle upon it. A tiny, hunched woman was cooking over an open fire. It reminded Gabriel of the simplicity of the O'Donnells place. A sense of wellbeing washed over him. Finley felt no such sense of peace. There was no sign of her father.

Davit introduced his mother to the visitors, and she gave a toothless smile. The small group watched respectfully as Davit took the 'Light of the World' from Finley and lit the candle on the table. Too old to have made the hike to the church, the tiny woman stood and prayed. Gabriel held Finley's hand, and they were moved by the woman's faith.

"Mama Franziska," Davit said, pointing.

The little woman was delighted to have a house full of people, but Finley could tolerate pleasantries no more. She took Mama Franziska's hand and bent down to look at her.

"Please," Finley said in a shaky voice, "Mon père?"

She pointed to a corner, partitioned with a curtain. Not a sound came from the other side of the fabric. Was her father too weak to even recognise her voice? Finley gulped.

"La."

Gabriel led Finley to the curtain, then opened it slowly, determined that he would shield her from the worst. He saw a man lying on a bed. He didn't move. His leg bandaged was raised, resting on a cushion. A warm sheepskin covered the rest of him. She let go of Gabriel's hand and walked toward the man. Gabriel watched her. Oh, how he loved this girl who was so beautiful, brave, fierce, and loyal.

The man was clean, and although he had lost weight, he was clearly not starving. Davit and Mama Franziska had cared well for him.

Finley kneeled down in front of the war veteran. Ernest Harrington put out his hand and stroked her hair.

"Finley?" he asked, confused.

"Yes, Papa."

Tears ran down her face as she took his hand and kissed it.

"You have found me," he whispered.

"Of course, I did," she answered gently, stroking his face.

"What day is it, my girl? It's all been a blur since I was brought here. Weeks, I think."

Finley's heart wanted to break, and she put her arms around him and embraced him with all the love she had.

"It is Christmas Day, Papa," she whispered through her tears. "And we've come to take you home."

***

Other books in Christmas Chronicles series

The Christmas Songbird
Victorian London's Theatreland is no place for a young girl. Danger and temptation lurk behind the bright lights and the applause.

Suzanna, the daughter of an unmarried costume seamstress, is used to being overlooked and rejected. Yet, as she grows up in The Songbird Theatre, she dreams of becoming a famous singer - but dreams are often shattered.

Talented and optimistic, she hopes for a bright future. Alas, her secret love for the wealthy theatre owner's son means she risks everything if discovered, especially as a jealous rivalry with another starlet intensifies.

Will the treacherous diva ruin Suzanna's dreams of happiness? Or will the humble girl's loyalty, dedication and determination be rewarded with the love and respect she deserves?

Buy The Christmas Songbird

View all my books on Amazon.

(https://author.to/EmmaHardwick)

***

Please help more people find this book by leaving an honest review.

Many thanks,

Emma

Printed in Great Britain
by Amazon

31544614R00144